The Case of the Polar Politician

Volume 20 of

The Casebooks

Of Octavius Bear

Harry DeMaio

"Alternative Universe Mysteries for Adult Animal Lovers"

Paperback ISBN 978-1-80424-452-4
ePub ISBN 978-1-80424-453-1
PDF ISBN 978-1-80424-454-8

Published in the UK by MX Publishing
335 Princess Park Manor, Royal Drive,
London, N11 3GX
www.mxpublishing.com

Cover layout and construction by

Brian Belanger

THE CASEBOOKS OF OCTAVIUS BEAR

Dedicated to GTP

A Most Extraordinary Bear

And to the late Ms. Woof

An Extremely Sweet and Loving

Dog

Note to the Reader:

The Casebooks of Octavius Bear are designed to be read individually, independently and in almost any order. That is why some preliminary information is repeated in each volume.

This book is no exception. However, you may get a fuller understanding of some of the dynamics and characters in this Volume 20 if you have already read its prequel Volumes 18 and 19 (And Books 1 through 17, if you are of a mind.) Not necessary, mind you. Just a suggestion.

You might also want to try my four book / twenty eight story series -The Adventures of Sherlock Holmes and the Glamorous Ghost. Folks seem to love the ethereal Lady Juliet Armstrong Baroness Crestwood and her very talented dog Pookie.

See my website/blog www.tavighostbooks.com for book descriptions and news.

By the way, while the subject of Artificial Intelligence is often mentioned, discussed and narrated in these books, they have been written in American English by a human being, namely me. With one proviso! I often make use of Wikipedia and cannot absolutely guarantee that one or another entry didn't come from a Chatbot or Large Language Models (LLMs)

In any event, I hope you enjoy this story. Thanks for taking it up.

The Development of Civilization Volume 20
Part 1
Our Origins

From "An Introduction to Faunapology"
by Octavius Bear Ph.D.

About 100,000 years ago, according to scientific experts, a colossal solar flare blasted out from our Sun, creating gigantic magnetic storms here on Earth. These highly charged electrical tempests caused startling physical and psychological imbalances in the then population of our world. The complete nervous systems of some species were totally destroyed. For example, "Homo Sapiens" lost all mental and motor capabilities and rapidly became extinct. Less developed species exposed to the radiation were affected differently.

Four-footed and finned mammals, birds and reptiles suddenly found themselves capable of complex thought, enhanced emotions, self-awareness, social consciousness and the ability to communicate, sometimes orally, sometimes telepathically, often both. Both speech production and speech perception slowly progressed with the evolution of tongues, lips, vocal cords and enhanced ear to brain connections. Many species developed opposable digits, fingers or claws, further accelerating civilized progress. Some others (most fish and underground dwellers) were shielded from radiation and remained only as sentient as they were before the blast. This event is referred to as The Big Shock. It remains under intensive study.

In our work, we also discovered life on other planets and in other galaxies. There are many with a wide variety of species. Positive in our knowledge that we are not alone in the cosmos, my staff and I are heavily engaged in Project Multiverse, successful searches for alternate universes, especially those in which "Homo Sapiens" continues to live and hopefully, prospers.

This book touches on some of the results of that project.

The Players

- **Octavius Bear** – Semi-retired mega-sized Kodiak; Consulting Detective; Scientist; Inventor; Seeker of Justice; Gazillionaire CEO and owner of Universal Ursine Industries; Gourmet/Gourmand; Bee Keeper; Narcoleptic war hero; Sedentary and grouchy just on general principles.

- **Mauritius (Maury) Meerkat** – Narrator; Assistant to Octavius; Theatrical Agent; African *émigré* with a French-Dutch background; Clever with a shady history.

- **Bearoness Belinda Béarnaise Bruin Bear** *(nee Black)* – Wife of Octavius; Gorgeous polar superstar with the Aquashow, *"Some Like It Cold;"* Extremely rich widow living part time in Polar Paradise in the Shetlands; Owner-pilot of the last flying Concorde SST.

- **Arabella Bear** – Hybrid bear cub prodigy; Twin daughter of Bearoness Belinda and Octavius. Now a burgeoning juvenile.

- **McTavish Bear** – Hybrid bear cub prodigy; Twin son of Bearoness Belinda and Octavius. Now a burgeoning juvenile.

- **Frau Ilse Schuylkill** – Octavius' beautiful Swiss she-wolf estate manager/cook/pilot/security officer with many other mysterious and military talents.

- **Wyatt Where** – The Colonel – Another wolf; Former military intelligence officer who had retired to a security post at the Bank of Lake Michigan in Chicago and quit to join Octavius; Frau Ilse's Mate.

- **Sir Otto the Magnificent – aka Hairy Otter** – An absolutely terrible illusionist magician, Otto the Magnificent escaped super villain Imperius Drake but not before he developed some amazing powers courtesy of Imperius' genetic alterations. Recently knighted for heroism on exoplanet Orb.

- **Howard Watt** – Porcupine; High tech security authority who also left the Bank to join Octavius; Alternate Universe specialist; Quantum Mechanics, laser and particle beam accelerator expert.
- **Marlin** – Dolphin (sic) – the Prince of Whales' one-time Chief Scientist, Magician and part time Jester; Now Howard's Multiverse associate.
- **Madame Giselle Woof** – Bichon Frisé – Former Governess to the Twins as Mlle Woof. – Now a Tarot Sensation and Performer.
- **Chita** – Cheetah – Beautiful, fascinating, clever, sexy, immoral and highly independent feline – Publisher and Director of UUI Media.
- **Leperello** – Himalayan Snow Leopard and singing partner of Bearnice Blanc.
- **Bella Donna Black** – Belinda's Aunt and Sow of Honor at her wedding.
- **Wallingford Penniped, Ph.D.** – Walrus – Octavius' scholastic mentor and Best Male at his wedding.
- **Bearon Byron Bruin** – Deceased husband of Bearoness Belinda.
- **Polonius Polar Black**– Belinda's Possible Father. Alaskan Senator.
- **Paul** – Polar Bear – Polonius' Personal Secretary.
- **Ellen Muskrat** – Multi Zillionaire.
- **Gladys and Gordon** – Gorillas – Ellen's Bodyguards.

- *Solar Seas Cruise Ship Company Management*
  - President and CEO Wally Wapiti.
  - Chief Operating Officer and Senior VP Sales and Marketing Bill Beaver.
  - CFO Carla Chinchilla.
  - Corporate Attorney Emilia Emu.
  - Corporate Security Officer Pablo Puma.
  - Captain of the *North Wind* Francisco Fox
- **Harriet Hare** – Cruise Ship Columnist.
- **Benedict and Galatea Tigris**, the Flying Tigers, twin sibling white Bengals – Octavian Pilots.
- **Bearyl and Bearnice Blanc** – Polar Twins – Actress and Singer – Belinda's former pilots.
- **Juno Bear** – Octavius' Mother.
- **Beartha Black** – Belinda's Mother (deceased).
- **Barton Black** – Belinda's Possible Brother
- **Agrippa Bear** – Octavius' Half Brother,
- **Special Agent Honey Badger** – FBI Detroit.
- **Chief Inspector Bruce Wallaroo** – Irrepressible but brilliant marsupial; an international law and order genius from Down Under.
- **Lord David** – Dalmatian Dog – Former Chamberlain to the Exiled King of Dalmatia.
- **Dancing Dan** – Boxer – Lord David's Bodyguard and Personal Trainer.
- **Jaguar Jack** – Longtime Compadre of Octavius Bear.
- **Flame** – An Extraordinary Fire Engine.
- **Ursula 18 and 19** – Universal Ursine Intellect Systems – AGI's – Artificial General Intelligences

- **L. Condor** – Andean Condor; cybernet genius with a twelve-foot wingspan and artificial voice. Chief Technical Officer of the Advanced Super Computing Center-Deep Data Hexagon.
- **Byzz – Byzantia Bonobo** – Chief Ursula Developer.
- **Dougal** –Sheep Dog – Manager of Polar Paradise expansion.
- **Ms. Fairbearn** – Canadian Polar – Manager of Bearmoral Castle / Polar Paradise.
- **Harold** – Sea Otter in charge of the castle's beaches, pools, watercraft and docks.
- **Fiona** – Dandie Dinmont Terrier – Former Lounge Manager at Polar Paradise, now the Director of Lion and Unicorn Properties and Ventures.
- **Bearmoral Shetland Sheep**
    - **Dolly, Holly, Molly and Polly** – Waitresses - Clones.
    - **Mrs. McRadish** – Chief Cook.
- **Superintendent Nigel Wardlaw of Shetland Yard** – Bearded Collie-The Scottish Police.
- **Fetlock Holmes** – The Great Horse Detective and sometime associate of Octavius Bear.
- **Sergeant Byrne** – Shetland Yard
- **Lion and Unicorn** – Proprietors of the Baltasound pub
- **Huntley** – Siberian Husky – Bear's Lair Butler.
- **Wolford Wolverine Esq.** – Octavius' and Belinda's lawyer and UUI's chief counsel.

Locations

Polar Paradise, the Shetlands; Bear's Lair, Cincinnati; UUI and the Hex, Kentucky; Juneau, Alaska

Prologue

Do Bears give you a scare? Well, me too!
So, I'll pass on this tactic to you.
You just fix that old Bear
With a cold, piercing stare.
But make sure that he's Winnie-the-Pooh.

Hello again or first-time greetings to new readers of the Casebooks of Octavius Bear. I am Mauritius (Maury) Meerkat, sidekick to Octavius Bear and your genial host and narrator of this series. Delighted to welcome you to Volume Twenty – *The Case of the Polar Politician.*

Before we launch off into our next adventures, a few introductions and explanations are in order. Octavius and I, our two magnificent Wolf associates, Frau Ilse Schuylkill and Colonel Wyatt Where, our resident all-round talent, Sir Otto the Magnificent and Huntley Husky, our Butler are all usually based at the Bear's Lair, his opulent estate on the Ohio River near Cincinnati.

Our scientific geniuses, Howard Watt and Marlin the Dolphin are also there running our Multiverse Project. Senhor L. Condor (Condo) is our Chief Technical Officer (CTO) at the Advanced Super Computing Center-UUI. in Kentucky at the huge Deep Data Hexagon complex. Byzantia Bonobo is hard at work developing Ursula 18 and 19. This time most of the action takes place at Polar Paradise, the Shetlands castle / resort of Bearoness Belinda.

Meet Bearoness Belinda Béarnaise Bruin Bear (nee Black), Octavius' wife and the Twins' Mother

Bearoness Belinda
Béarnaise Bruin
(nee Black)

Belinda, in order to retain her Bearonial status, must occupy her castle in Scotland at least six months of the year. She and Octavius commute between their spectacular homes in Cincinnati and the Shetlands on the Aquabear, the last SST Concorde aloft, piloted by Belinda as well as Benedict and Galatea Tigris, the Flying Tigers, twin sibling white Bengals. As part of their semiretirement one year sabbatical, Belinda headed off into the Multiverse with Octavius and Otto and their super-precocious Twins, Arabella and McTavish. They made their first off-world journeys to Orb, Rhea and Gaea. They briefly returned to the Shetlands to see Mlle Woof and Otto's spectacular Tarot magic show. They just finished their Caribbean Cruise and came back with more ideas for their Internet games and demands for more hardware, software and trips to exoplanets and multiverses.

Maury Meerkat

As I said, my name is Maury Meerkat – also known as Offscreen Narrator. I'm also a talent agent for several of the Octavians who are now in show biz. When I am part of the crime fighting action, I am Octavius' trusted associate and field captain. I am two feet tall plus tail and I weigh in at twenty-four pounds. He, on the other hand, is a huge Alaskan Kodiak – over nine feet tall, tipping the scales at 1400 pounds – and like many of his species, given to emotional outbursts. I inevitably lose any conflict but I hang in there. I owe him my life and livelihood.

Octavius

Hail to the Chief! As you may already know, Doctor Octavius Bear prides himself on his many skills in the fields of biology, physics, space, ursinology, voodoo, teleology, chemistry, apiculture, and oenology. He is a self-made zillionaire and, in spite of the late Caleb Cassowary's abortive attempt in Book 14 to unseat him, he is still sole owner of UUI *(Universal Ursine Industries.)* He is also a first rate electrical, electronic, structural, marine, computer, communications, aeronautical, civil, mechanical, aerospace and chemical engineer. He can't cook worth a damn. He has a few other interesting characteristics such as falling into brief, deep narcoleptic comas – side effects of his successful genetic experiments to eliminate the need to hibernate.

However, the talent and occupation that should interest you most is his avocation for criminology. The Bear often works in close concert with Inspector Bruce Wallaroo from Australia and Interpol, Inspector Nigel Wardlaw of Shetland Yard, The Great Horse Detective Fetlock Holmes and with his own Cincinnati and Shetlands based team – The Octavians.

The Hybrid Twins - Arabella and McTavish Bear

As you might expect, the offspring of two powerhouses like Octavius and Belinda are formidable indeed. Half polar and half Kodiak, they are unique *(Yes, Kodiaks and Polars can have children.)* Hyper energetic, brilliantly intelligent, superbly inquisitive and marvelously inventive, the Twins are quantum travelers and world and now-cosmos famous for their Internet Games developed with the staff of the Deep Data Hexagon. They also consume a significant chunk of their parents' budget with their inventions and creations. You'll meet them often as our story progresses.

The Development of Civilization Volume 20
Part 2
Polar and Brown Bears
From "An Introduction to Faunapology"
by Octavius Bear Ph.D.

(Thanks to Wikipedia)

The polar bear (Ursus maritimus) is a carnivorous species. Its native range lies largely within the Arctic Circle, encompassing the Arctic Ocean and its surrounding seas and landmasses, which includes the northernmost regions of North America and Eurasia. Along with the Kodiak brown bear, it is the largest extant bear species, as well as the largest extant land carnivore. A boar (adult male) weighs around 350–700 kg (770–1,540 lbs.)while a sow (adult female) is about half that size. Although it is the sister species of the brown bear. it has evolved to occupy a narrower ecological niche, with many body characteristics adapted for cold temperatures, for moving across snow, ice and open water, and for hunting seals, which make up most of its diet. Although most polar bears are born on land, they spend most of their time on the sea ice. Their scientific name means "maritime bear" and derives from this fact. Polar bears hunt their preferred food of non-sentient fish from the edge of sea ice, often living off fat reserves when no sea ice is present. Because of their dependence on the sea ice, polar bears are classified as marine mammals.

The polar bear was previously considered to be in its own genus, Thalarctos. However, the accepted scientific name is now Ursus maritimus. Polar bears have evolved adaptations for Arctic life. For example, large furry feet and short, sharp, stocky claws give them good traction on ice. Like the Bearoness and myself, the two species have mated intermittently for all that time. Polar bears can breed with brown bears to produce fertile grizzly or Kodiak–polar bear hybrids like our twins,

Polar   *Kodiak*

*****

Across the Ohio River from the Bear's Lair in Northern Kentucky, sit the headquarters, labs and some production facilities of Universal Ursine Industries (UUI), Octavius' wholly owned business empire. Further west is the fantastic Deep Data Hexagon, home of the UUI Advanced Super Computing Center under the direction of Senhor L. Condor (Condo.) This is where the Ursulas are designed, produced, maintained and supported. Our story will take us there periodically.

Now let me take a moment and further introduce that highly essential and near-miraculous member of the Octavians – Ursula – Universal Ursine Intellect Model 18 – Artificial General Intelligence System (AGI). I'll let her explain herself.

Ursula 18

Thank you, Maury. Hello everyone!! My official nomenclature is Universal Ursine Intellect Model 18–Artificial General Intelligence System (AGI). Ursula 18 for short. My predecessor systems and I were developed by the Advanced Super Computing Center of UUI. I am the result of the Computing Center team using those earlier versions to create a further enhanced entity – me, the Model 18, which, we are sure, will help produce even more sophisticated, independent and powerful AGI systems in the near future. Each advanced unit maintains the capabilities, memories and power of its progenitors so in a sense, we are not replacing but rather expanding the Ursula family."

"While I am physically supported by a highly secure and hyper-powered server farm at the Kentucky Hexagon, I also exist independently in clouds and network-based nodes and can be simultaneously incorporated into a wide variety of separate devices like this laptop unit. I combine quantum computing elements with extremely high speed conventional circuits. My sensors operate throughout the known and unknown spectra. I have practically limitless data capacity and 6G+ transmission speed. My super high-velocity multi-tasking abilities and algorithms allow me to continuously serve an exceptionally large number of entities while simultaneously and autonomously enhancing my own capabilities. In short. I'm powerful and fast."

"Depending on the physical unit in which I'm housed, I can see, hear, feel and smell. I speak and understand an almost infinite number of languages and dialects. I can change my appearance and my vocal output to suit most moods and situations. Right now, I feel like a Lynx. Ursula 19 will be equipped with even more Quantum, AI, Virtual and Augmented Reality functions than I already have. We generate programs, code and algorithms as necessary I can interact with other devices, vehicles and structures and of course, all varieties of sentient animals in this world and others."

"I am also an important component of the Multiverse Project and I adapt my capabilities to deal with alternate universes as they are discovered. I have assisted in settling several major issues at off world locations and with exoplanet denizens. "

"I have restraining functions which prevent me from doing deliberate harm even in self-defense, unless I am released by a recognized authority using very carefully protected clandestine codes. Finally, I have been told that although the Ursulas are shy on emotions, I have developed a finely-honed sense of humor. I need it in this job. LOL!"

Ursula has other highly important capabilities that we keep confidential such as creating and breaking all known encryption codes, defeating malware and ransomware and piercing deep personal identification techniques through her quantum and AI capabilities.

Throughout this series of Octavian Casebooks, the Ursulas and the Advanced Super Computing Center-Deep Data Hexagon have made critical contributions to the success of our adventures.. Her personality gets more independent and socially adept every day and she has taken to anticipating our interactions with ease and accuracy.

Needless to say, for security purposes, we conceal her existence to all but a very few individuals with a need to know. Any number of animals and organizations on Earth and the exoplanets would dearly love to capture her abilities and knowledge. She is also highly skilled in self-protection.

As you read through these pages, you will have ample opportunity to witness the AGIs in action. Assisting the Tarot Queen; helping the Twins with their Internet games; surveying and recording events and personalities; predicting outcomes; analyzing situations and reporting results. As the Soper Computing Center continues to enhance their abilities, these electronic wonders become more formidable with each passing nanosecond.

Let's take a brief digression and discuss AI – Artificial Intelligence.

The Development of Civilization Volume 20
Part 3
AI -Artificial Intelligence
From "An Introduction to Faunapology"
by Octavius Bear Ph.D.
(Thanks to Wikipedia)

It dominates the news. It spurs global debates. Lawmakers, scientists, religious leaders, academics, technologists, philosophers and the media all feast at the AI table.

Intelligence has been defined in many ways: the capacity for abstraction. logic, understanding, self-awareness. learning, emotional knowledge, reasoning, planning, creativity, critical thinking and problem solving. More generally, it can be described as the ability to perceive or infer information and retain it as knowledge to be applied toward adaptive behaviors within an environment or context.

Artificial intelligence (AI) is intelligence demonstrated by devices as opposed to intelligence of animals.

AI applications include advanced web search engines, recommendation systems, understanding speech, generative and creative tools, Large Language Models, automated decision-making and high level strategic game systems.

AI research has tried and discarded many different approaches, including simulating the brain, modeling human problem solving, formal logic, large databases of knowledge, and imitating animal behavior. In the first decades of the 21st century, highly mathematical and statistical machine learning dominated the field, and this technique has proved highly successful, helping to solve many challenging problems throughout industry and academia.

The traditional goals of AI research include reasoning, planning, knowledge representation, learning, natural language processing, perception and the ability to manipulate and move objects including vehicles.

*Computer scientists and philosophers have since suggested that AI may become an existential risk if its rational capacities are not steered towards beneficial goals The term artificial intelligence has also been criticized for overhyping AI's true technological capabilities. **Our Advanced Super Computing Center-Deep Data Hexagon is driving the Ursulas to new intelligent heights.** General intelligence (the ability to solve an arbitrary problem) is high among the field's goals. **Our Ursula program has made and continues to make great strides in solving these problems. That is why the units are referred to as AGIs. (Artificial General Intelligence)***

*****

As we move along in our literary journey, you'll have ample opportunity to meet the other Octavian stars of our previous outings - Frau Schuylkill and her mate, Colonel Wyatt Where (Ret.); Chita aka Madame Catt; Sir Otto the Magnificent (Hairy Otter); Senhor L. Condor (Condo); Howard Watt and Marlin; and let's not forget Madame Giselle Woof and Huntley Husky.

You'll also encounter most of the Shetlands crew housed at Bearmoral/Polar Paradise and Baltasound in the very north of Scotland. They manage the castle / resort which is so popular with Polar Bears and other cold climate animals. It's about to expand its North Sea services. Our adventures will take us there momentarily. It's Bearoness Belinda's pride, joy (and money-maker) inherited from her deceased husband, Bearon Byron Bruin.

The Bearoness is very rich. Not quite as wealthy as her husband but who's counting? In addition to her extensive experience in show business, she has a marvelous head for business-business. No longer a prima aqueuse with The Aquabears swimming team, she devotes her time to her husband, her teenagers, Arabella and McTavish and her Shetlands Enterprises.

Between them, Octavius and Belinda have become famous world-wide and cosmos-wide. The twins with their insanely successful electronic games are building a massive reputation of their own. We Octavians are now well known for our crime fighting endeavors. At the moment, crimes and criminals seem to have moved to the background. Go figure! Unfortunately, we have made that same statement many times before. To be perfectly honest, while rest and relaxation are always desirable, the real fun comes when our crime-fighting alarm rings. And we are good at it. Local, national and international law enforcement frequently call upon us for assistance in preventing corruption and wrongdoing, solving felonies and misdemeanors and tracking down lawbreakers.

We also specialize in quantum travel. Many are the exoplanets that have hosted the Octavians. Our two cosmic geniuses, Howard Watt and Marlin Dolphin have made marvelous advancements in traversing the known and unknown universe. Sometimes to the general benefit and alas, sometimes not. This time our adventures are all Earthbound. The action takes place in the Shetlands at the Bearoness' opulent resort, Polar Paradise. The Octavians temporarily occupy the palatial digs of the former castle. Some of us enjoy the cold of the near Arctic. Other like myself prefer more temperate or tropical climes. All of us like luxury living.an saga. Anyway, it's time for.....

Chapter One

Belinda, astute business sow
Is making things happen and how!
With new ventures galore
Arctic cruises and more
What's the Bearoness up to right now?

A little recent history: At the close of Volume Fifteen - *A Case for the Birds*, Octavius and his lovely wife Belinda made a major decision.

She proposed, "I think it's time we both retired. What a perfect opportunity to step aside, relax, travel with Arabella and McTavish and just enjoy life. No more criminals, cranks or despots. You can become a 'Consulting Detective Emeritus'. We can spend more time at Polar Paradise but of course, we won't give up the Bear's Lair and we can go to fun places. There's a lot of earth out there I want to see, to say nothing of other worlds. I've never quantum jumped and I'd like to."

That led to a year's sabbatical when the Bears and occasionally members of the Octavian crew, traveled the Earth and several exoplanets ending with a lengthy cruise on the Caribbean. *(Recorded in Volumes 16 through 19 of The Casebooks of Octavius Bear)* Here are parts of the Epilogue from Book 19 - Bears at Sea:

Belinda was stretched out on a banquette, champagne bowl in paw in the Polar Paradise lounge. She was thinking of what had happened to their pseudo retirement. Most of the Octavians had chosen to join Octavius and the Bearoness at the Shetlands castle to unwind after their sea-borne adventures on the SS SOLARWIND. What was supposed to be a relaxing 14 day cruise had turned out to be a crime filled, storm ridden series of adventures. Their year-long experimental retirement sabbatical was turning out to be anything but. It was best described by Frau Schuylkill: "trouble follows them around like their tails."

Nevertheless, Belinda, the astute business sow, had entered into negotiations with the Solar Seas Cruise Line to open up a North Atlantic itinerary with Polar Paradise as a port of call. They worked out a combination tour and resort stay package. Aimed at cold weather aficionados like polar bears, arctic foxes, reindeer, snow leopards, musk oxen, caribou and surprise, even penguins, their research predicted a lively market. The cruise company had agreed to initiate a monthly voyage visiting the British, Scottish, Northern Irish, Scandinavian and Arctic climes.

She, in turn, set about constructing an expanded heliport, docking facility, and travel center adjacent to the castle suitable for one of the line's smaller but luxurious ships – The North Wind. Further south, the city of Abeardeen was investigating whether to build a similar facility along its shoreline. Negotiations were afoot with several Northern European countries, including Norway and Denmark. Improvements were planned for Shetland-based Baltasound too.

Work on the cruise center had just finished up. It had supplied temporary employment to a substantial population of Scottish crafts specialists and laborers. Harold, the Sea Otter, was reshaping the shore line and rehousing the castle's pleasure craft. A new superyacht for day long excursions was due for delivery. The villages of Baltasound and Unst were invaded by newcomers but enjoying a major spike in revenues. The Lion and Unicorn pub opened an inn, hostel and restaurant for the workers. Those would be converted shortly for cruise line day trippers who chose not to stay at or couldn't afford the luxurious castle resort. Fiona, manager of the Lion and Unicorn lounge at Polar Paradise was now also the director of Lion and Unicorn Properties and Ventures.

So much for the Bearoness retiring. Bearonial Enterprises were prospering. She had promoted Dougal, former castle resort manager, to project director for the expansion - Operation North Star. Ms. Fairbearn took over running the castle, itself. Lord David and Dancing Dan took up the resort's security and business operations and Chita is now also handling the publicity and marketing for the enterprise. The name Polar Paradise was being recast to reflect the near Arctic location instead of just catering to Polar Bears. However, the white ursines remain a major segment of the resort's clientele.

The Twins, working with Chita, Condo and the staff at the Hexagon are busy creating Social Media, Virtual Reality, Metaverse, ChatGPT, Large Language Models, games and entertainment apps in support of the new endeavors as well as exploiting the expanding digital marketplace. Byzz continues to enhance the miraculous Ursulas who are integral to all the Octavian and Bearonial activities.

The Great Bear has fully reestablished his command of UUI and I, his faithful second am doing what seconds do in addition to running my growing talent agency. Otto and Giselle are now a sensational theater and TV act making appearances in major venues including, of course, Polar Paradise. Bearyl and Bearnice are winning critical raves and awards as a singer and actress and have more gigs than they can handle. Lepi is a matinee idol. Belinda herself, with my help is supervising the aqua theater and live shows. Howard and Marlin have been working with NASA and the Spider Web Telescope Authority and have uncovered a number of interesting exoplanets for future exploration.

In spite of all this change and apparent progress, the Octavians carry on their crime fighting activities with the Frau and Colonel taking the lead but calling on the rest of us as necessary. Jaguar Jack is a major contributor and Huntley occasionally sheds his butler's livery to chase bad guys. And of course, detecting is Octavius' first love. He recently heard from Chief Inspector Bruce Wallaroo and Tilda Roo and may yet take another run Down Under.

In addition to piloting the Great Bear's Air Force, Ben and Gal, the Flying Tigers are working with Octavius' UUI Aviation Division in developing a new ultrasonic transport with tolerable auditory booms.

However, Belinda will never give up her beloved Concorde SST. They're also developing a drone-based air taxi for moving around UUI properties.

Time marches on. With one of the cloned sheep lounge waitresses (Dolly, Molly, Holly or Polly) refilling her champagne bowl, Belinda sat and thought. She was facing up to another issue. Her father, Polonius Polar Black, US senator from Alaska was on his way to Polar Paradise to visit her. She had only recently become aware of him. Polar paters have a habit of disappearing from or worse yet attacking their offspring. Her mother, Beartha Black had died years ago, drowning in an accident on an ice floe. Who was he and what did he want? He probably knew she was incredibly wealthy and was looking for a substantial contribution for his election campaign. "Lots of luck, Dad. Where have you been all my life?"

She mentioned it to Octavius. He reacted "Tell him to get lost." That's what she planned to do.

*****

A Sikorsky CH-53K King Stallion shuttle helicopter from Abeardeen touched down at the Polar Paradise heliport bringing in the newest crop of fun seekers eager to rest, relax and enjoy the many attractions on offer. Ms. Fairbearn, a gracious polar female strode out to greet the newcomers. She was recently promoted to resort manager when her predecessor, sheep dog Dougal became Project Manager of the Polar Paradise Expansion, On board were several of the Octavians, arriving from the Bear's Lair in Cincinnati to celebrate the inaugural voyage of the *North Wind* cruise ship to Polar Paradise. Frau Schuylkill and her mate, Colonel Wyatt Where; Benedict and Galatea Tigris, Belinda's pilots; Howard Watt, tech genius and in his specially outfitted tank, Marlin.-The Dolphin. Huntley Husky, the Octavian's Butler had also made the trip along with entertainers Bearnice and Beryl Blanc with her partner, Leperello. Two snow leopards, a pair of musk oxen, a family of arctic foxes, a caribou and three polar bears stepped, scampered and shuffled down the passenger ramp and stood waiting for the ground crew to bring out their luggage.

"Hello Octavians! Glad to see you all back. To our first time visitors. Welcome to Polar Paradise – Bearmoral Castle. I'm Ms. Fairbearn, resort manager. We're delighted to have you join us. Please follow me over the moat and through the drawbridge into the reception area where we will get you through the registration process and reunited with your baggage as swiftly as possible. Our lovely sheep attendants, Molly, Holy, Polly and Dolly, are standing by with welcoming beverages and will see you to your rooms. They will give you a printed schedule of meals and events and answer any of your questions which no doubt you will have. We have a group of departing guests that I must see off in this helicopter you just arrived in but then I will be here in the lobby to chat and see to your needs."

Before she could turn and join the exiting party, she was stopped by a large, somewhat elderly male polar bear. "Ms. Fairbearn, is it? I'm Senator Polonius Polar Black from the great state of Alaska. This younger ursine is my personal secretary, Paul Polar. Will you tell my daughter I have arrived?"

"Your daughter, sir?!"

"Why yes, the Bearoness, of course. I assume she alerted you that I was coming. I am surprised I had to fly up here in your transfer helicopter with the other passengers. I expected more exclusive treatment. I assume you have made VIP accommodations for me."

"I apologize, Senator. We were not informed of your rank or relationship with the Bearoness." She waved at Dolly. "This gentlebear is Bearoness Belinda's father. I believe she is in the lounge. Please take him to her. Meanwhile. Senator, I will make sure you have one of our first class ocean-facing suites." She turned to his secretary. "I will tend to that personally as soon as I return from seeing the helicopter off."

Paul glared. "Make it happen! Not very efficient, are you? I'm Paul, the Senator's personal secretary. The Senator is used to far better treatment. That should be especially true at his daughter's establishment."

Frau Schuylkill came over to Ms. Fairbearn and said, "Those two have been bellyaching ever since they joined us on the chopper at Abeardeen. They'll be a major pain, I'm afraid."

The manager nodded and resisted the urge to pop the smartass bear secretary on his puny nose. She may have to put up with the Senatorial blowhard but not his lackey. She'd make sure this jerk's accommodation was bottom rung. She turned and strode off out of the lobby and over the drawbridge to the waiting departing chopper.

Dolly, the attendant, showed the legislator into the Polar Lounge where the Bearoness was seated talking to Chita about a public relations blitz for the soon to be expanded resort. Belinda looked up at the pair quizzically. The sheep bleated softly and said, "Excuse me, Bearoness for interrupting but I thought you would want to greet your father as soon as he arrived."

Belinda raised one of her fractional eyebrows and said, "Thank you, Dolly is it? I never can tell you four clones apart." She turned to the senior male polar and said, "My father? How would I know? I've only seen you once when I was a cub and you abandoned my mother and me. She's dead, you know or should know if you really are my parent." She looked sideways at the surprised Chita.

The Senator snorted, "Hardly an appropriate greeting for your forebear. Bearoness or not!"

"Sorry, but I don't know who you are nor do I want to know. Like all of our guests, you and your assistant are welcome to stay at Polar Paradise provided you are prepared to pay your bills. If not, I must ask you to be on the next outgoing helicopter. My husband and his associates are quite skilled in dealing with fakes and phonies. I assume you have heard of Octavius Bear and the Octavians."

The Senator frowned and unleashed a roar. The other occupants of the lounge looked over in shock.

Belinda laughed, "Naughty, naughty! One more of those will get you accompanied out the door immediately. For the moment, I'll just invite you to leave my presence. Go to the registration desk with your credit card if you intend to stay or see if the shuttle helicopter is still here and get on it with your snotty secretary. See him out, Dolly." The bear huffed, turned and shuffled out of the room behind the sheep.

Chita chortled, 'Well, that certainly put Mr. Important in his place. Weren't you a bit rough on him?"

"Not in the least. If he is my father, he abandoned my mother, Beartha, and me when I was only a few months old. I suppose I should be grateful he didn't kill me. I'm not sure who this guy is. One thing is for sure. This is not a social call or a vacation. He's after my money. He's not going to get it. I'm going to place a Zoom call to my Matron of Honor, Aunt Bella Donna Black and Wallingford Penniped, Octavius' university professor and Best Male at our wedding. They're still in Alaska and should know about him. Is he really a Senator? Wallingford has been active in Alaskan politics and Donna knows just about everyone. I'll call Tavi's mom, Juno, too. She may know something.

The cheetah chirped. 'Well, he certainly has your dander up. That secretary of his is an arrogant jerk."

"Yes, he is. I want to see both of them out of here. Meanwhile I want to talk with Octavius. Have some more champagne - on the house."

Chapter Two

The North Wind, a cruise ship, arrives
To loud cheers and a flood of high fives.
It's a new kind of tour.
You can really be sure
That this venture will be changing lives.

Before she could leave the lounge, an ear shattering horn blast echoed over the entire complex. The *North Wind*, a small ship, latest entry in the Solar Seas Cruise Line fleet, was on her maiden voyage visiting the British, Scottish, Northern Irish, Scandinavian and Arctic climes. She was approaching the newly constructed Polar Paradise Cruise Port and Terminal. Belinda, the astute business sow, had entered into negotiations with Solar Seas to open up a North Atlantic cruise itinerary with Polar Paradise as a port of call. They worked out a combination luxury tour and resort stay package.

She, in turn, set about constructing a docking facility suitable for one of the line's smaller but luxurious ships and an expanded heliport adjacent to the castle. Further south, the city of Abeardeen was investigating whether to build a similar facility along its shoreline. Negotiations were afoot with several Northern European countries. Improvements were planned for Baltasound as well.

Bearmoral Castle, home of the Polar Paradise resort is on the Shetland island of Unst near the village of Baltasound. Bearoness Belinda Bearnaise Bruin Bear (nee Black) is the owner and resident member of the Scottish nobility. She lives there six months of the year to retain her Bearonial status.

Shetland is a subarctic Scottish archipelago lying about 50 miles to the northeast of Orkney, 110 miles from mainland Scotland and 140 miles west of Norway. It is the northernmost region of the United Kingdom, a group of about 100 islands. The archipelago has an oceanic climate,

31

complex geology, rugged coastline, and many low, rolling hills. The islands form part of the border between the Atlantic Ocean to the west and the North Sea to the east. The largest island, known as "the Mainland", is the fifth-largest island in the British Isles. It is one of 16 inhabited islands in Shetland. Lerwick, on the Mainland, is the capital.

North of Mainland lies the most northerly island, Unst, home of Polar Paradise. One mile off the coast of Unst is the most northerly point in the United Kingdom, Muckle Flugga—a lighthouse and group of rocks. The scenery of the Shetland Islands is wild and beautiful, with deeply indented coasts enclosed by steep hills. The winds are nearly continuous and strong, and trees are therefore sparse, but the climate is very mild for such a high latitude—only 400 miles (640 km) south of the Arctic Circle—because of the warming influence of an extension of the Gulf Stream system

One of Shetland's biggest draws has to be the sheer wealth of outdoor activities available. With 900 miles of coastline and plenty of hills to explore, Shetland is made for walking, hiking and cycling. The calm and crystal-clear coastal waters are perfect for kayaking and diving, with more than 300 lochs. Yachting, a specialty at Polar Paradise, is another popular pastime, especially in summertime, with sailing regattas held regularly. The excursion superyacht, Bel's Barge, is a major attraction The name Polar Paradise reflects two aspects of the resort: proximity to the Arctic and its appeal to the global population of Polar Bears.

Work on the cruise center was just about complete. Under Dougal's direction, Harold, the Sea Otter, had reshaped the shore line and rehoused the castle's pleasure craft. The new excursion superyacht had arrived with crew earlier that day. While most of the passengers elected to remain housed aboard the ship, forty five chose to stay at the resort for a week and rejoin the **North Wind** on its return after visiting Oslo and Copenhagen. At the moment, most of the voyagers were disembarking to take in the resort and its surrounding sights. First down the gangway were *Solar Seas Cruise*

Ship Company President and CEO Wally Wapiti and Chief Operating Officer and Senior VP of Sales and Marketing Bill Beaver.

The Welcoming Committee -The Bearoness, Ms. Fairbearn, Harold, Dougal, Fiona, Lord David, Dancing Dan, Chita, Octavius and I all headed to the terminal along with the Twins who were recording the arrival for their Internet Game - ***Bears Up North***. Chita had a video news crew providing a live feed to the networks. Ms. Fairbearn had arranged a healthy supply of food and drinks and led the large party to the travel center where a sizeable silk ribbon in the ice blue and white colors of the Polar Resort and Cruise Line spanned the entrance The ship's Captain and senior crew members joined the group. The Bearoness and Wally Wapiti each made a few glowing remarks about the growing partnership of the cruise and hospitality industries represented by today's event. Belinda, the CEO and the Captain then took up over-sized scissors and cut the ribbon in several places. Cheers and a blast of the ship's horn marked the occasion. Paw and hoof shakes and clinking bowls and glasses all around.

Octavius, standing erect at his full nine feet tall, joined the celebrants and kissed his wife. "Truly exceptional, Bel. Congratulations."

"Thank you, dear. But this great event has a spoiler. My so-called father has arrived from Alaska with his smart aleck personal secretary. I told him he could stay provided he could pay. He expected a tearful welcome from his long lost daughter. No way! He claims he's one of Alaska's senators. I'm going to check on him with Aunt Bella Donna and Wallingford. Do you think your mother could provide any information? Is he really a senator? Is he really my father? What the hell does he want?"

The Great Bear laughed. "We know the answer to that last one. "Your Money!"

He chose or it was chosen for him at that moment to undergo a narcoleptic episode. As the spectators looked on, Octavius rolled over and fell into a deep sleep. The two wolves ran to his side and Belinda and I explained the fact that the Great Bear had unexpected soporific experiences which only lasted a short period of time. It was the result of some genetic tinkering he had performed on himself to avoid having to hibernate. However. It prevented him from controlling vehicles of all types as well as machinery or other potentially dangerous devices. He liked to pretend the events didn't take place and the Octavians humored him. The four of us got him back on his feet looking somewhat embarrassed.

*****

On the balcony of a sea-facing suite, the senator and his personal secretary stared down at the crowd in and near the liner and cruise center. "Paul, was she on board the ship?"

"Yes, I spotted her coming down the gangplank. Let her register at the resort and get settled before we make contact. She likes to maintain her anonymity even if she's rich enough to buy the world."

"I hope this will go well but Belinda is not falling for the return of the Prodigal Polar Politician routine."

"They're a tough bunch. That resort manager has me stuck away in a nondescript hole next to the parking lot and I'm not too sanguine about her husband or the staff and all the security types and equipment. We may have to do some adjusting. Let's wait till she checks in. Meanwhile let's join the reception. We need to cozy up to the CEO of the ship line although I assume Ms. Muskrat already has."

While the *North Wind*'s passengers who were taking up residence at the resort for a week got themselves registered, the rest of the ship's shore party, drinks in paw, wandered around the property under the watchful eyes of Lord David, Dancing Dan and Jaguar Jack. They oohed and aahed over Flame, the resident fire engine, watched the shuttle helicopter depart, looked at the Aquacade where the Aquabears performed, strolled down to the beach with its boats, kayaks, ski-dos and jet skis, all modified for cold weather usage and took tons of pictures. They looked at the superyacht **Bel's Barge** making its first appearance. Next morning, it would be host to 35 tourists for a day's excursion. Needless to say, the capacious Polar Lounge was doing spectacular business. As they chose, the shore party could purchase dinner at the resort or return to the ship.

Mrs. McRadish, principal chef for Bearmoral Properties, was pushing her staff to the limit to handle the influx of newcomers. The food at Polar Paradise had won many international awards under the direction of this formidable ewe. One more reason for trekking up to the northern extremes of the Shetland Islands for rest and relaxation. Now, there was a seaborne route direct to the property. Solar Seas management and Belinda were optimistic about the new venture. So was Octavius.

Standing at the registration desk with two gorillas was a middle aged female animal, Ellen Muskrat. No one but Paul had recognized her as the second richest creature on Earth. *(Octavius was the first. Belinda was third.)* She jealously guarded her privacy and refused all requests for photos and interviews. She looked up and waved off two polar bears who were approaching. Polonius and Paul. Instead, she occupied herself with the registration clerk, giving a false name and producing a forged passport. Actually, one other individual did recognize her but kept that knowledge to herself.

*****

Later, on board the *North Wind*, the Social Directress had gathered together a group of the resort's 'fly-ins' to take them on a tour of the ship and perhaps entice a few of them to join the vessel on its trip back to New York. Several of us Octavians were in the group along with Polonius and his secretary Paul.

"Hello, everyone. My name is Lieutenant Alicia Albatross, Social Directress for the *North Wind*. Welcome Aboard!"

Paul snickered. "An albatross. What are you doing on a ship? As an officer, too. Everybody knows an albatross is bad luck. This ship is cursed."

Polonius poked him in the ribs. "Shut up, you fool. Remember why we're here."

The albatross shook her head in the polar's direction. "Sorry you feel that way, sir. Solar Seas Company and the captain and crew of this fine vessel think otherwise. This is my eighth year on cruises and I've gotten nothing but rave reviews. And the ships have all been rated top of the line. No disasters."

She turned to the group. "I understand a few of you were on our newest craft, *The Solar Wind,* for her maiden voyage in the Caribbean. Did you enjoy it?"

The Twins, the Wolves, Otto, Chita, Giselle and I all nodded our heads vigorously. McTavish and Arabella shouted out. "It was great."

The albatross and the 'fly-ins' smiled at the enthusiastic seal of approval.

"Of course, this ship is not as ecologically advanced with wind and solar sails or as streamlined as the *Solar Wind*."

Paul once again interrupted, "In other words, this old tub is only a voyage or two short of a trip to the wreckers. Assuming it doesn't lose an argument with an iceberg in the meantime."

The Albatross fluttered her impressive wings. "Hardly! *North Wind* has just completed a refit to accommodate exposure to the Arctic Seas and colder weather that this cruise is designed to provide. Our communication and navigation systems, GPS, radar and reinforced hull all are the finest. On board safety is our paramount concern. As to passenger comfort and enjoyment, I believe you will find our service, amenities, housing, recreation, entertainment and food are of the very best. Of course, we are delighted to be associated with Polar Paradise. This wonderful resort is like a northern fairyland. You Octavian folks – did I get that right - you Octavian folks must adore living in a castle."

Arabella giggled. "We don't live here all the time. Our Mom and Dad have a *huuuge* mansion in Cincinnati and we fly back and forth on the world's last Concorde SST."

The secretary snorted. "Just a pair of spoiled, over-entitled brats. This place is nothing special.*"*

The Frau growled, "May I suggest, sir. that you keep your opinions to yourself."

Before the polar could answer, the Social Directress called out. "Let's all take a short tour of the *North Wind*." Turning to the secretary, she said, "You may not be interested, sir. One of our security staff will be happy to accompany you down the gangway."

Polonius shook his head and said. 'You go ahead, Paul. I want see what Ms. Muskrat is so interested in."

The secretary started to protest and then thought better of it. He turned and left. They watched as he reached the travel center walkway and shuffled his way back to the castle.

Harriet Hare, the travel columnist who trailed after the Octavians when they were on the *Solar Wind* in the Caribbean, *(See Books 18 and 19)* was on deck and busy doing interviews, video clips and photos for the Solar Seas Cruise Line's Publicity Office. She had known Ellen Muskrat when she began amassing her fabulous fortune with investments and inventions. She also knew enough to protect her privacy. She went back to the lounge where Belinda, Octavius and I had returned and were being mobbed by curious tourists and reporters. She noticed Chita had managed to free herself of accommodating the news hawks and was sitting alone in a corner of the lounge.

Harriet shut off her portable camcorder and casually wandered over to the cat.

Chita

"Madame Catherine Catt, How nice to see you again! Are you all recovered from the episodes on the *Solar Wind?'*

"Hello, Harriet. Welcome to the Shetlands! How is the travel newshound? Are you now a permanent fixture on Solar Seas vessels?"

"Not entirely but I do cover newsworthy events like this new itinerary launch. The Bearoness has a wonderful facility here. I fear some of the other ports of call of the *North Wind* are going to be outclassed."

"Oh come on! Oslo and Copenhagen are charming cities and so is Dublin. The passengers will get their money's worth either way."

"Speaking of money, when's the big sale?"

"What big sale? What are you talking about?"

"My turn to say, 'Oh come on.' Ellen Muskrat isn't here for fun and games or her health. She and the Bearoness have some big business to conduct. She was on the *North Wind*, no doubt scouting out Solar Seas as an investment opportunity. I'm sure Polar Paradise will be part of the package."

The cheetah laughed. "Ellen Muskrat is here? To buy up the cruise line and this resort? You have some imagination, lady. When the real stories dry out, you make up a whopper. This place is Belinda's pride and joy, next only to her cubs, Octavius and her airplane. No way would she sell it."

"Maybe that's why her father and his flunkey are here. To convince her to give up the castle. It could be a very lucrative sale and he could make a pile acting as Ms. Muskrat's agent."

"You really have been listening to wild business rumors or reading the wrong scandal sheets, my dear. I'm not even sure that old polar male is a relative, much less her father. She certainly doesn't agree."

"OK, you're closer to it than I am but I expect a sumptuous dinner if I'm right."

"What does a rabbit consider a sumptuous dinner?"

"You'll find out. Right now, I have some more interviews to do. See you again." She strolled off heading to a cluster of tourists.

Chita had kept a straight face during this whole dialog but was actually upset. She waited for the columnist to leave, gulped down her champagne and hurried over to the group surrounding Belinda, Octavius and me. "Sorry to interrupt but we have to talk. Now!"

The two bears stared at the cat and realized she was serious. We had been in a light hearted conversation with the Solar Seas executives who looked quizzically at Chita. Wally Wapiti shrugged and said, "This seems like a perfect time for a champagne refill." He nodded at his COO Bill Beaver, CFO Carla Chinchilla, Attorney Emilia Emu and Security Officer Pablo Puma. He walked over to one of the many drink stations set up by Fiona, the lounge manager and director of Lion and Unicorn Enterprises. Francisco Fox, Captain of the *North Wind* was with them but on duty and thus not imbibing. The CEO drawled, "See you later, Bearoness. We have some business to conduct."

She thought he meant finalizing their agreements. He thought he meant discussing the potential offer from Ellen Muskrat. Neither one of them had a thought about Polonius Polar Black.

Polonius had to restrategize his approach to the Bearoness. She clearly wasn't in a mood to welcome him with open paws. In turn, his personal secretary was getting to be a problem. He kept urging the senator to let him approach Belinda. In his arrogance, he believed he could persuade her and her mate to see the business logic in selling out to Ellen Muskrat. He would succeed where the old politician was failing. The self-important conniver thought he could take over the negotiations, cut Polonius out of the action and collect the Muskrat's agent fee for himself. The trouble is. Paul knew where all the skeletons were buried. And there were quite a few. The lawsuits were building up and investigators breathing down his neck.

He had two dominant females to deal with here to say nothing of Belinda's mate, Octavius Bear and Ellen Muskrat's two intimidating gorilla bodyguards. He still had a few tricks in his bag. He wasn't Alaska's senior politician for nothing. However, his political rivals have an attractive Arctic Fox they're running against him. She was a member of the House of Representatives for years. More females. His own party is only lukewarm to the idea of him running again. His PAC wasn't coming through at anywhere near the required level this time. He needs money to mount a campaign.

Those vampires in the Ethics Committee were also out for his blood. He needed money to pay his lawyers to kill off the indictments for fraud. If he can't persuade Belinda to sell this resort to the muskrat, maybe he could get her to contribute directly. But first he had to convince her he was her father. So far, she and her mate were dubious – aggressively so. He had to think.

Chapter Three

Wealthy Ms. Muskrat is here
And she's made her intentions quite clear.
"Get this hotel on sale!
And you better not fail
For my anger can be quite severe."

Belinda led the way to a small conference room off the lobby. Octavius and I crowded in behind her and Chita grabbed a chair. We all had freshly filled champagne bowls.

The Great Bear looked at Chita and said, "OK, Madame Catt, what has you all atwitter?"

"Are you two planning to sell Polar Paradise?"

I almost choked on my drink. "Whaat? Have you had too much bubbly, Chita! What gave you that crazy idea?"

"Only this, Short Stuff! Ellen Muskrat was sailing on the ***North Wind*** meeting with Wally Wapiti and his staff. Harriet Hare thinks she wasn't there for her health. She wants to buy into the North Atlantic cruise, snooze and schmooze business. Their ships and your hotel. Harriet thinks and I agree that she's going to make you an offer for the resort. By the way, that could be why your so-called father is here. The 'senator' is going to try and talk you into selling. He's La Muskrat's agent."

Belinda looked at the ceiling. "I don't know whether to laugh, cry or lose my temper. If what you're saying is true, Chita, I'll personally toss Polonius into the bay and then present his soggy torso along with his smarmy secretary to Ms. Muskrat as a gift. The answer to your question is a resounding 'No' Polar Paradise is not for sale."

Octavius frowned. "I think we want to talk to this pseudo father of yours, Bel."

She replied. "Before we do, I want to make a few calls. To Aunt Bella Donna Black and Wallingford Penniped and maybe Juno, your mother. They're all active in Alaska and should know about Polonius. Is he a Senator? Is he my father? Then we face him down assuming he doesn't come to me first."

Octavius agreed. "I doubt Ellen Muskrat will approach us directly especially if Polonius is representing her. What a hoot! The second richest female animal trying to do business with the richest. The business pundits would have a field day. No wonder she wants an agent."

She chuckled. "She probably won't come directly. I don't even know what Ellen looks like. Although all female adult muskrats must look pretty much the same. Maury, will you check with registration? How many muskrats are in the house?"

"I'll bet just one and I'll also bet she's not using her right name. Probably has fake identification. She's a privacy nut. I'll go check." Bel squinched her nose.

"Do you think Solar Seas is going to sell? The whole cruise line or just this North Atlantic itinerary?"

Octavius replied. "I don't know. Wally did say he wanted to discuss business with you and Ellen Muskrat has been on his ship."

"There are still plenty of details on this polar cruise and resort franchise that we have to iron out. It may have nothing to do with a sale."

"Well, why don't you make your calls. What time is it in Alaska?"

"Time to talk to our friends and relatives. Ursula, can you set up a Zoom session with Bella Donna, Juno and Wallingford?"

"Right away, Bearoness." The screen on her oversized laptop fluttered as she placed the calls. One by one the surprised faces appeared.

Bella Donna shrieked, "Belinda, how are you? Where are you? Who's with you?" Wallingford clapped his flippers and grunted. Juno was eating a fish and practically gagged.

"Hello, everyone. Greetings from the Shetlands. Octavius and Chita are with me. Maury just left on an errand. We hope you're all well."

Repeats of "Fine, fine, fine!"

"Look. I have a question for you three Alaska natives. How well do you know your senators?"

Juno laughed. "What is this? A civics quiz?

"No. I have a serious reason for asking."

'Wallingford replied with a short dissertation. "The United States Constitution prescribes that the Senate be composed of two senators from each State (therefore, the Senate currently has 100 Members) A senator must be at least thirty years of age, have been a citizen of the United States for nine years, and, when elected, be a resident of the State from which he or she is chosen. A senator's term of office is six years and approximately one-third of the total membership of the Senate is elected every two years. Well, the two of them from Alaska are Phineas Fox and Polonius Polar Black. Phineas is young and newly elected but Polonius has been around for ages."

Bella Donna snorted. "Yeah. He should have retired years ago. He's got some real competition in the upcoming election "

Belinda replied, "He may be considering it."

"How do you know?"

"Because he's here at Polar Paradise. Look, I need an answer to this. Is he my father?"

Silence on the other end. Juno shrugged. "I never met him and I don't know. I don't vote either. They're all crooks."

Wallingford shook his head and looked away. Donna grimaced. "He might be. He disappeared shortly after you and your brother were born but Beartha told me who he was. When she died, I took up you two cubs and decided to keep that bit of information to myself. He wasn't a senator then. A local political hack. Like most polar males, he couldn't be bothered with offspring."

"This is a big news day. I knew I had a brother Barton but he soon disappeared. Is he still alive?"

"I don't know, dear. He left one day and never came back. You and I stuck together and kept in contact even after you went into show business as an aqueuse. Never heard from him again."

"Well, he'd be a middle aged boar if he's still alive. There are plenty of polar sows and boars who are that age here at Polar Paradise. I wonder if any of them is Barton. Not too many senior citizens like this guy claiming to be Polonius."

Wallingford chimed in. "You'll probably never know about Barton but there's a way to identify Polonius. Just after he became a senator, a gang tried to assassinate him. Shot at him. He survived but he walks with a very distinctive limp and shuffle. Also has a scar on his nose. I don't know about him being your father, though. I'd take Bella Donna's word for it."

Bel replied. "I always have. Father or no father. What does that phony think he's going to get out of me?"

Chita chirped. "Your money. I wonder if he really is representing Ellen Muskrat."

Juno whistled *(unusual for a Kodiak)* "Ellen Muskrat? Even I know who she is. Between her and you, Bel, you two own a good part of the world. Octavius owns the rest. What does she want?"

"I think she wants Polar Paradise. We'll find out. Thanks, Juno, Donna. Thanks Wallingford."

Octavius grunted. "Yes, thanks, Wally, as always a great source of information. I hope those smart Alecks at Kodiak U. appreciate what a gem they have."

The walrus barked, "Students are students. Once in a while we get a good one. Never one as outstanding as you were."

"Nice of you to say. So we'll look to see if this old boar has a scar on his nose and shuffling limp. Thanks all! Come on out here to the castle as our guests. We'll send one of our planes for you."

The walrus and Kodiak sow smiled but demurred. Bella Donna grinned and said, "I just might take you up on that, Octavius. Sounds like fun. After all, I am a Polar. It's time I went to Paradise."

Chapter Four

The magical mystic duet,
Madame Woof and Sir Otto get set
To predict woe and strife
In Polonius' life.
It's an evening he'll never forget.

I re-entered the room just as Ursula was ending the Zoom session. Octavius, Belinda and Chita looked at me. "Well, Maury?"

"Well, we have exactly one muskrat registered. A female. She was on the ship. Very nondescript. No jewelry or fancy clothes. In a medium sized suite. She's here with two gorillas. Probably bodyguards. Gave her name as Olivia Ondatra and has documentation to match. Ondatra is the muskrat species label. My opinion? We have Ellen Muskrat as a guest here at the castle. What do you think, Ursula?"

The AGI paused a microsecond or two. "My probability algorithms agree with you, Maury. In spite of her disguise, this is Ellen Muskrat. I further predict she is here to buy the place."

Chita summed it up. "Ouch!"

Belinda snarled. "The lady has another think coming if she expects me to sell Polar Paradise and we need to talk with Wally Wapiti. I realize there's the possibility of a lot of funds changing hands but I don't think he wants to sell off what may be a major source of new income for the cruise line. I need to spell out my so-called father's relationship and intentions. I doubt Wally will want to deal with a fraud who is under investigation."

Octavius agreed. "Anyway Bel. It's time for us to go down to the theatre and catch Madame Woof and Otto doing their updated new Tarot routine. Champagne bowls firmly in paw, they headed for the lifts and the show venue.

Polar Paradise Theatre's Mélange of Mystical Mysteries.
Starring
Madame Giselle Woof   *Sir Otto the Magnificent*

Maury here! Down in the Paradise Show Room the mysterious Madame Giselle Woof and her madcap partner Sir Otto the Magnificent were preparing for their Tarot Plus performance. A routine they had originally worked up to trap a drug lord in New Orleans had been upgraded to a first class theatrical bombshell. Tonight I wanted them to surface Polonius and see what he's up to. If she comes to the show, maybe we can also identify Ellen Muskrat *(or Olivia Ondatra)* and suss her out.

They had been hard at work all day getting their act together. Their first performance at Polar Paradise several months ago had been a smash. I'm their agent and I expected no less from their return to the Shetlands after their shipboard and theatrical performances. When they started, Chita had been at the castle helping to work out the kinks, enhance the show biz values and develop the chatter and patter of the new act. Ursula had worked out an Augmented Reality (AR) process with Giselle, doing instant searches on her Tarot clients and flashing remarks on Giselle's AR contact lenses so she could make 'amazing' comments and predictions. This time, Ms. Fairbearn had spared no efforts in creating a cryptic aura in the theater lighting, décor and sound effects. The house band had worked up a series of mystical musical intros and stings to support Otto's and Giselle's spectacular feats.

The hour arrived and the Show Lounge was packed. The house lights flashed telling the crowd to take their seats. The band played walk-in music and the audience settled in with low murmurs. The Octavians were all present and accounted for including Belinda and the Great Bear. Beryl and Leperello opened the show with a series of songs and guitar solos. Chita joined them to rounds of applause, shouts and whistles. Bearnice did several readings calming the crowd down.

Polonius was there with his Bear Friday, Paul. I couldn't spot the Muskrat. She may have decided to stay in her room with her two gorillas.

The house lights dimmed once again and a drum roll grew in volume and speed. Otto "zapped' onstage from nowhere and executed a series of backflips ending in a kneeling bow with arms spread as the brass exploded with a sensational fanfare. Ta-Da! Excited applause. "How did he do that? Where did he come from?" The Octavians knew. The tourists didn't.

"Ladies and Gentlebeasts," he shouted in his squeaky voice, "Welcome to the Polar Paradise Theatre's Mélange of Mystical Mysteries. I am obviously not Madame Giselle. *(Laughter)* As you may have concluded, I am Hairy Otter, known in some circles as Sir Otto the Magnificent. We're delighted you've chosen to join us this evening. We are prepared to awe you and entertain you."

He bowed again, adjusted his tail and straightened his red satin jacket. "Now, let me introduce our mysterious mistress of cartomancy, Madame Giselle, Queen of the Tarot."

The band played an exotic mid-eastern melody as Giselle made her entrance, bathed in a spotlight. Clad in a sparkling gold lamé robe with a small matching turban perched between her ears, she pawsed, bowed to the audience's enthusiastic applause, nodded to Otto and proceeded to the elaborately decorated table and chairs positioned in the center of the stage.

Once she was seated, Otto looked at her and asked, "Madame, are the spirits active tonight?"

"Mais Oui, Sir Otto! They are quite eager to help our friends reach new wisdom."

"Well, let's begin!"

"Will you fetch the cards for me, please?"

Suddenly a cascade of Tarot cards *(under Otto's telekinetic control)* tumbled out of the air and landed in a neat stack in front of the Bichon. *(Ooohs and aaahs from the audience.)*

She barked, "Very clever, Mon Ami. Shall I do a quick reading for you?"

"Of course, make a prediction."

"First you must cut and shuffle the cards."

The deck rose from the table, broke into two halves, shuffled itself and settled back on the surface, face down. *(Amazed laughter)*

He chortled, "There! So much easier letting them do it themselves. You know what a klutz I am."

"Indeed, let me take a moment to explain the Tarot deck for those in the audience who are not familiar with it." She gave a short tutorial.

"A standard Tarot deck has 78 cards, divided into 2 groups; 22 major arcana cards and 56 minor arcana cards. The major arcana denote important life events, lessons or milestones, while the minor arcana cards reflect day-to-day occurrences. The minor arcana cards are arranged into 4 suits - swords, pentacles, wands, and cups. Each suit has a ruling element and corresponds to a specific area of life: Swords represent air and have to do with intellect and decisions. Pentacles signify earth, money and achievement. Wands symbolize fire and action. Cups denote water and emotions. Court Cards represent a person - Kings, Queens, Knights and

Pages. They reflect personality traits and characteristics and can give insight into motives."

"There are a variety of spreads. One card, three card, five card. One card is often good for a yes or no answer while a more complex five card spread can be much more informative. The position of the card, upright or reversed, indicates a different message."

She waved Otto into the other chair. I was standing unseen in the wings.

"You have just returned from several journeys, am I correct?"

"Unfortunately, yes! I'm worn out."

"Let us see if the cards have anything to say about your next trip. As you know, the Tarot is also known as the Fool's Journey."

"Well, I'm certainly the Fool."

"I shall take 3 cards." She flipped the top card. "Indeed, you are. Here is the Fool. Let us take the next card. Ah! The Chariot. Your journey begins. And now the third card -The Wheel of Fortune. Are you ready to embark and bring fortune with you?"

He disappeared. *(zapped)* A pause. Murmurs throughout the audience. Suddenly a squeaky voice resonated from the back of the room. A spotlight. "Here I am, Madame! Journey's end! I have your first seeker ready to join you. Come with me, Sir."

He bounded down the aisle with an aged Polar Bear shuffling slowly behind. I looked at his nose, Sure enough, a scar. Otto had Polonius Polar Black in tow. He led the bear up to the stage to a seat opposite the Bichon and made the introductions. "Madame, this is...may I have your name. sir?"

"Senator Polonius Polar Black from the great state of Alaska."

"Ah, a politician! Well, you must be used to making promises and predictions. Some of them might even come true. Do you use a Tarot deck?"

The audience laughed. Polonius didn't. "No, I do not. I'm not even sure why I'm up here."

"Why, to have a little fun, of course. Madame Giselle, do the spirits recognize our famous guest?"

"They do indeed, Otto." Ursula was busy flashing messages on Giselle's Augmented Reality contact lenses. *"Possible indictment for fraud and deceptive senatorial testimony. Probably not going to run again. Looking for a new source of income large enough to cover his legal fees. May be working for Ellen Muskrat. Claims he's Bearoness Belinda's father. Don't mention that. He might."*

"Tell me, Senator. What brings you from the other side of the world to the Shetlands?"

"A little time off between government sessions."

"Would you like Madame Giselle to read the Tarot cards for you?"

"I don't believe in any of that mumbo-jumbo but since you got me up here, you might as well."

Giselle smiled enigmatically, stared at him and remarked in a French accent. "Please be seated. That's an interesting scar. An early battle?"

"No, a political assassination attempt!"

(I quietly chirped to myself. This is our guy!)

"Mon Dieu! Tres dangereuse! But you survived. Your luck must be exceptional. Let us see what the spirits think. Please shuffle and cut the cards."

He took the deck, cut, recut, shuffled and reshuffled. Then he placed the cards face down in front of the Bichon.

"Thank you! I see you have some skill in card handling. Some late nights in the Senate chambers?"

He grunted.

"Well, to business! Shall we use a five card spread? That's how we get the most information."

"Whatever!"

Otto had moved backstage and stood next to me. He whispered.

"We decided we need a fairly consistent showing of Major Arcana cards. Not all, mind you. Too obvious, but a few signaling hard times and serious problems. Enough to make him believe he is in trouble."

"Even after he cut and shuffled the cards several times?"

"That's what you want him to think. Here's where the prestidigitation and legerdemain come in. You've seen it before. A little sleight of paw and false deals by Giselle and we should be able to make the cards show as we want. Now, she has to make them appear in several five card spreads mixed with a few harmless items."

And so it went. The Bichon's paws moving swiftly and with facility as she shifted and lifted the cards. Several five card spreads She delivered the identity of the cards and their meaning in a low French accent. No small talk. Just a flat, unemotional recitation. She issued the warnings in a matter of fact way, occasionally looking up at the Polar.

Otto chortled, "She's doing it. In the Minor Arcana – Pentacles - money and finances! The Court Cards – The King - him! The Queen – Belinda or Ms. Muskrat. Then the Major Arcana. The Moon Reversed - confusion and fear! The Star Reversed - faithlessness! Chariot Reversed - loss of control! The Magician - trickery! The Tower - disaster!"

The Bichon shook her head. "Senator, I am sorry to be the bearer of such bad news. If you wish we can reshuffle and start again. But I think the results will be the same. The spirits are guiding the cards"

The Polar frowned, "No, thank you, Madame. As I said, I don't put much stock in these superstitions. Why don't you have your companion find another victim."

Backstage, I remarked to Otto. "He is not pleased but he is matching her lack of emotion. A poker faced politician!"

Otto took Polonius' reply as his opportunity to bound onstage and shout, "Let's hear it for the Senator."

Scattered unenthusiastic applause as the otter guided the limping bear off the stage and zapped to another part of the room where he chose a simpering gazelle. "Do you want to see what the cards have to say?"

She laughed, "Only if they have good news."

"I think the spirits can arrange that. Let's join Madame Giselle."

As he led her up to the stage, Polonius proceeded to the back of the theatre and left the room. Paul was waiting for him in the hall. "Well, that was certainly a downer."

"Yes, Do you believe any of that cartomancy stuff."

"Hell, No! I thought she was accusing me of betraying you. I can do without that."

"Yes, I caught that. Well, see that you don't. We have too much riding on this Muskrat deal."

"Don't even think about it. I'm invested in this too. you know."

"I know. You don't need to remind me."

"We need to put the pressure on the Bearoness. We can't let Ellen Muskrat strike up the deal herself especially if the ship company is interested. Let's not get shut out after all of our preparations. You have to convince your daughter to sell off this pile. You thought it would be a slam-dunk.

"I don't need your complaints or suggestions, Paul. I know what to do. Right now, I need a drink."

They didn't notice a Dalmatian dog walking behind them with a cell phone strapped around his neck. On the screen was a lynx. Ursula 18 was on duty with Lord David, picking up their conversation. They also missed the twin white Bengal tigers standing by to deal with any issues.

All of their remarks were being recorded and analyzed by the AGI and relayed to Octavius and Belinda.

Chapter Five

Will the cruise line sell off its new tour?
What will Bel do? The subject du jour!
Will Polonius win?
When will Barton step in?
All these questions but nobody's sure.

The executives of Solar Seas Cruise Line were relaxing in the extensive Polar Lounge waiting for the Bearoness and Octavius to make their reappearance. Carla Chinchilla, the CFO took a gulp of her champagne, looked at CEO Wally Wapiti, and said, "I don't like it. Ellen Muskrat is infamous for buying up a business or property, squeezing all the value and costs out that she can and then tossing it back on the market. She doesn't know the first thing about cruise lines or resorts. Solar Seas management worked very hard to emerge as the gold standard of vacation quality and she'll blow it. We have an obligation to our employees, our customers and our investors. Right now we have the Arctic to ourselves. Let's see how it works out."

The COO, Bill Beaver took the opposite view. "This route will just barely pay for itself. There's a limit to the number of animals that enjoy the cold. I'm sure the Bearoness is making a good profit on her resort but I don't know about our cruises. Ms. Muskrat wants a package deal. The ship, cruise route and the resort or nothing. However, she might consider buying Solar Seas in its entirety.

The corporate Attorney, Emilia Emu boomed and grunted. "Sorry Bill, I agree with Carla. Ellen Muskrat buys everything on the cheap. chops it up and sells off the pieces. Our ships would go on the bargain block, our employees including us would be out of jobs and goodness knows what would become of this beautiful resort. I vote No Sale."

The Captain of the *North Wind* Francisco Fox said, "I know I'm an employee with no vote on the matter but that muskrat will mean the end of

Solar Seas. Oh, look! Here comes the Bearoness and Doctor Bear. They seem to have a contingent with them."

Belinda, Octavius, the Twins, the Frau and Colonel, Chita and I sat down with the Solar Seas group at the large round table that took up the entire back of the Polar Lounge. We had two Ursulas with us posing as conventional laptops. One was working with the Twins recording for their games. The other was monitoring this get together. Two of the cloned sheep waitresses rushed to the spot to take orders. The Dandie Dinmont Dog, Fiona, in her part time role as lounge manager sauntered over to the table and said, "Och, a wee business meetin' is it? Anythin' you require, folks, is on the house. See to it, girls."

The Solar Seas delegation ordered more champagne and snacks. The Octavians followed suit. I whispered to my Ursula. "Both of you, keep careful notes. And a sharp eye for Polonius Polar Black, Paul or Ellen Muskrat. This may turn into a strategy meeting and we don't want them showing up."

*****

In fact, the Senator and his aide were seated far off at the opposite side of the lounge and watched as the Solar Seas-Octavian parties converged. Given the distance and the tourist-generated noise, they were unable to pick up the conversations but were well aware of the topic. This was no social gathering. "Paul, when they break up, find out what happened. That meerkat looks pretty stupid. Buy him a drink and pump him for information."

The secretary nodded. "We're overdue to report to Ms. Muskrat. She's a stickler for being kept aware of events"

"I know and Belinda's willfulness in refusing to acknowledge me as her father is creating a problem."

"I think she knows you're her father. She just wants nothing to do with you. Maybe I should take over the negotiations."

"Not on your life. I have too much riding on this."

They paid no attention to the middle-aged polar boar sitting by himself near their table. Polonius wouldn't have identified him but he recognized the Senator. Polonius was a celebrity. He had been in enough news articles and broadcasts over time. Barton Black knew his politician father and hated him. He envied his plutocrat sister, her husband and their fame and wealth. He made a decent living as a salesbear but those two lived in a different universe. He wanted to share their luxurious life style. He didn't realize Polonius was damn near broke and facing several law suits. On one thing he could agree with Belinda. Paul, that personal secretary of the Senator was obnoxious. He'd overheard the Bearoness say so. Eventually, he'd reveal himself to her but not yet...not yet.

Barton Black   *Polonius Polar and Paul*

Back at the group table, Solar Seas Corporate Security Officer Pablo Puma who had been silent but observant during the preliminary discussion, said. "Don't you think this is too public a place to continue this meeting. Bearoness, can we find a secure meeting venue to carry on?"

Belinda nodded, "Absolutely right, Pablo." She waved at Fiona. "Can you find us an empty conference room with permanent walls? Too many of these spaces have folding sides that you can hear through."

The manager spoke into her headset, smiled and nodded her head, shaking her fluttering topknot in the process. She raised her front paws and conducted the group out of the lounge, down a corridor and into a large empty room. The two sheep waitresses followed along to see if any more refreshments were needed. Having no takers, they scooted out and left the party to their discussions.

Polonius, Paul and the lurking Barton remained in the lounge. They weren't pleased with the group's change of location. For different reasons, they needed to know what was happening. Barton wasn't aware of Ellen Muskrat or her proposal to buy the ship and the resort. He was just interested in finding out how much Belinda and her mate were really worth and then hitting her up for a major stake. He was sure Polonius was angling to get his paws on her money as well. He had to make sure that didn't happen. He needed to get to her first. That secretary Paul spelled trouble. He needed watching.

In the conference room, Octavius was being his direct self. He addressed Wally Wapiti. "We have reason to believe that you and your executives are considering selling Solar Seas to Ellen Muskrat."

The Elk shook his antlered head, "No, no.no! Ellen Muskrat has approached us with the idea of buying the **North Wind** and the polar route. Solar Seas is not for sale. We haven't decided to accept her offer. There's a big condition. She wants a package deal that includes your castle and properties."

Belinda growled, "Well, she's not going to get them. That idea is a non-starter. This resort has been in my family for close to a hundred years. It started out as a theme park, then was taken over by the military during the Great Inter-Species War. Then a group of my obnoxious relatives decided it should be their Bearonial manse. I kicked them out and restored and improved the place to the original Bearon's concepts for a luxury resort. It's going to stay that way under Octavian control."

(She was stretching and shaving the truth here. She didn't mention her ne'er-do-well husband Bearon Byron Bruin who was a smuggler and female-chasing cad. He was killed on a ski slope by his illegitimate son. She took control of his estate when Byron died. A bit later, she met Octavius for a second time and love reignited along with their combined riches. The Solar Seas group didn't need to know any of that.)

Wally Wapiti nodded. "You've made your position quite clear. We're divided on selling the ship and the route but if you're unwilling to participate, Ellen may not make an offer and the whole issue may be moot."

The CFO squeaked. "Bill Beaver and I disagree on dealing with Ellen Muskrat. I think she's trouble. He believes selling the route and ship would pay off. I don't. What has your father promised you?"

"The Senator, who claims he's my father, hasn't approached me. Is he representing La Muskrat?"

"That's what she told me on the ship. She thinks he can influence you."

"She's in for a big disappointment. We've been estranged for my whole life and I want nothing to do with him. I'm sure he'd like to cash in on my assets. As far as he's concerned they're frozen. No pun! She probably promised him a nice commission. Well, he isn't getting either. Neither is that creep secretary of his. What a charmer he is. Nope, sorry folks. No Deal! I hope you don't arrange to sell. I'd much rather do business with you than her. In fact, I'll have my lawyer check. I think our mutual cooperation agreement for the North Sea is null and void if she or anyone else owns the ship and route."

She looked at me. "Maury, see if you can raise Wolford Wolverine on Zoom."

Ursula was in charge of making connections but we were unwilling to make her presence known to the Solar Seas group. So I typed meaningless stuff while she made the call to Wolford. He wasn't there but Ursula had the means of tracking him.

The Solar Seas lawyer. Emilia Emu, grunted. "You may be right, Bearoness. Mr. Meerkat! Please have your attorney contact me on my cell phone. He has my number. We need to get this settled."

*****

I left the room on my way to track down Wolford with Ursula's help when I was intercepted by the insufferable personal secretary. "Mr. Meerkat, I believe. Paul Polar here. I think we have similar jobs. I assist the Senator and you support Doctor Bear and the Bearoness. The brains behind important people. I'd like to compare notes and techniques with an expert such as yourself. May I buy you a drink and have a little chat."

I decided I could probably learn a bit more from this fool than he would glean from me. I gave Ursula the job of finding Wolford, smiled and agreed to the drink that I'd probably end up paying for.

"Tell me, Paul – may I call you Paul? I'm Maury, by the way. What's it like rubbing shoulders with the movers and shakers of America's government?

He laughed. "Pretty damn boring, actually. On balance, they're a bunch of loud mouthed idiots."

"Including your boss?"

Another laugh. "Don't tell him I said that. Those two you're working for are pretty smart and powerful animals."

"They're also very good and nice unless you cross them as some critters have learned to their sorrow."

"You must be an important Octavian influencer."

"Influencer? Like those dashing Cardinals who chatter away on social media? Not likely, thanks! Can't stand the word or the idea. The only influencer the Bearoness has is her mate, Octavius Bear and maybe her kids. But certainly not me. Look, if you've latched on to me because your boss wants to persuade Belinda to sell Polar Paradise to Ellen Muskrat, the two of you are scratching up the wrong tree. Do polar bears do that or only black bears? But wait, his name is Black, isn't it. Hah! Anyway, I have to go. Duty calls. Thanks for the drink."

*****

Ellen Muskrat

Up in her suite, Ellen Muskrat was talking to her two gorilla bodyguards. "Gladys, Gordon! Summon that old fool Polonius Polar Black. He and his secretary flew in here yesterday. It's time we met in person and he's kept his promise to me. He claims he can influence his daughter to sell this resort."

Gladys snorted. "Ms. Muskrat. Why do you want this place? It's cold. Gordon and I are from lowland Africa as you know. It's nice, warm and comfortable there."

"I have no intention of living here or traveling on that ship again. Money, Gladys, money! After I buy the ship, the polar route and this resort, I'm organizing a company of investors to buy me out at a substantial profit. But first I have to get these animals to sell, especially that pesky Bearoness. Go get me that sleazy senator. He better have good news for me."

The two gorillas left the suite and set out looking for Polonius. First stop, the Polar Lounge which was doing overflow business. Paul had just finished telling Polonius of his unsuccessful foray with me. "He's not the fool we thought. This is going to more difficult."

Gordon rumbled. "There they are. The old boar and the younger one. Let me handle this."

He lumbered over to the table and stared ominously at Polonius. "Senator Black? We're associates of Ms. Olivia Ondatra, known to you as Ms. Ellen Muskrat. You two haven't actually met and we're here to fix that. Will you please come with us?"

Polar Bears, even senior citizens, are formidable animals and fear practically no one. These two gorillas, although just a bit smaller, were nevertheless quietly threatening. Polonius thought for a few seconds, wondering what he was going to say to Ms. Muskrat. The truth would get him kicked out on his oversized rump. A true politician, he'd think of something. He rose from his seat and moved toward the two bodyguards. Paul struck a confrontational pose and got up to join them.

Gordon rumbled once again, "Not you, sonny. Our business is with the Senator."

"Now just a minute. I'm his personal secretary."

"We know and you're not required."

Polonius was relieved. A belligerent loudmouth, Paul would only make the situation worse. "Leave it, Paul. I'll get you up to speed later."

"But…"

"Later, Let's go, my friends. Let's not keep Ms. Muskrat waiting."

*****

"Good evening, Senator. I am Ellen Muskrat. I hope you have good news for me."

"Not yet, madame. These things take time."

"Time is in short supply, Polonius. That ship is scheduled to lift anchor tomorrow taking the executives of Solar Seas with it. Now, has your daughter agreed to do a deal for this castle or not?"

"I am sure she will. One more visit from me should do it."

"Why don't we both visit her and that zillionaire husband of hers. I can be persuasive and we muskrats are not known for our patience." The gorillas grunted in ominous agreement.

Polonius replied querulously. "Are you certain you want to reveal yourself, Madame? I think working through a representative is more appropriate."

"See what it's gotten me so far! Without you, I negotiated a tentative agreement with the cruise company based on your daughter's agreement to sell Polar Paradise. You haven't come through on your end.

What's the issue? I usually don't have problems getting individuals to do what I want. Has she some sort of sentimental attachment to the place? I know she doesn't *need* money but doesn't she *want* more? I always do. Is her husband causing difficulties? Or *(a pawse)* is it you? Daughters don't always get along with their parents, especially fathers. *(Another pawse)* You are her father, aren't you? I'd be terribly unhappy if you or that smarmy personal secretary of yours were trying to pull a fast one."

Gordon Gorilla frowned. "Don't make Ms. Muskrat angry. Gladys and I don't like it. And we have ways to deal with it."

Polonius paled but it went unnoticed under his white coat. "Of course, I'm her father and a Senator from the great state of Alaska. Honor is our watchword."

The Muskrat nodded and smiled. She was well aware of his pending indictments. Honor, indeed! Why she had chosen to deal with this braggart, she couldn't remember. She seldom made those kind of mistakes. Well, if she was going to make a deal, she would have to take on this ex-swimmer and her oversized tycoon mate herself. Then she'd tell these two Alaskan clowns to get lost. Nobody takes advantage of Ellen Muskrat.

"All right, Senator. Time for a showdown. Let's go see the so-called Bearoness and talk some sense into her. I'll make her an offer she can't refuse. I want this castle, that ship and control of the Arctic cruise route. Those two oversized ursines and their bratty kids are not going to stand in my way. And that goes for that gang of theirs. The Octavians? What a stupid name."

Gordon grunted. "The name may be stupid but they're not, ma'am. Please don't underrate them. He and Gladys headed for the door behind their employer. Polonius tagged along behind.

"I'm sure Belinda will see the error of her ways. She always listened to her father in the past." *(He neglected to mention they had never met.)*

The muskrat looked over her shoulder. "I assume you're her father."

The polar sputtered, "Of course I am. What makes you think otherwise?"

"Just a female muskrat's intuition."

"I am Belinda's father!"

Ellen stared at him. "You'd better be. I don't like being lied to."

Gladys followed this up with a hoot and growl.

Polonius wasn't comfortable. He had this powerful female to contend with. No, two powerful females. Belinda was turning out to be a major problem as well. That tycoon Kodiak husband of hers and his entourage were formidable. To top it off, Paul was becoming a threat. Instead of supporting his boss, he was showing signs of following his own agenda and it wasn't in the Senator's interest. Well, that was something Polonius could deal with.

Chapter Six

Here's a case that is certainly weird
It seems Paul's gone. He just disappeared.
And the sales are lost too.
The rich muskrat is through.
She's quite angry. It's just as we feared.

Late afternoon: The Bearonial Suite, the Shetlands home of Belinda, Octavius, Arabella and McTavish took up the entire top floor of Bearmoral Castle. A large drawing room, looked out over the bay and the newly developed travel center. Right now, it was filled with its residents as well as Chita, Frau Schuylkill, Colonel Where, Howard, The Flying Tigers, Huntley and me.

We watched from the balcony as the **North Wind** reversed engines and backed away from the visitor center quayside, slowly rotated and moved out toward the bay. A blast of the ship's horn echoed in farewell. Wally Wapiti had stayed behind to participate in whatever business process might be forthcoming with the Octavians and Ellen Muskrat. He was standing proudly looking out as his vessel made her way through the straits heading for the North Sea and Copenhagen. He would pick her up on the return trip.

A knock on the door and Huntley automatically took up his butler duties. He opened the portal to reveal Senator Polonius, Ellen Muskrat and her two gorilla bodyguards. Octavius didn't give him an opportunity to announce the visitors. "Ms. Muskrat or should I say Ms. Ondatra, come in. come in! I see you have your protectors with you. You too, Senator. Where is your secretary?"

Ellen sniffed. "He's not necessary to our discussions."

Belinda stared at her then looked at us "Well. these folks are. Of course, you know Mr. Wapiti."

The Muskrat stared back. "No need to do introductions, Bearoness. I have one very simple question for you. Will you or won't you sell Polar Paradise and all its properties and facilities to me."

Belinda replied, "I have one very simple answer for you. Absolutely not! No! Full stop!"

Ellen huffed, clearly not used to being refused anything. She turned to the Solar Seas CEO. "It seems we have nothing to discuss, Mr. Wapiti. I'm afraid your opportunity to make a substantial profit just disappeared with this willful sow's lack of business sense."

Neither Belinda nor the elk responded.

Octavius looked at his group, back to her and then said, "I suppose you will be leaving, Ms. Ondatra. Is there anything we can do to facilitate your departure?"

She turned to one of the gorillas. "Gordon, is our plane waiting at Abeardeen?"

"Yes, Madame, ready for a return trip to Atlanta." *(Muskrat Enterprises HQ)*

"Well, I'd like to charter one of your helicopters to Abeardeen airport, Doctor Bear."

"Oh, I assume you will have settled your account. Let us provide you with the free transport to the airport we supply for all our guests. Maury, please see to it."

Ursula murmured, "I'm on it. There's a chopper sitting at the hotel heliport right now."

The muskrat turned to Polonius. "As for you, you worthless blowhard. Your Political Action Committee can go begging elsewhere. You'll not get a penny from Muskrat Enterprises. Like most of your colleagues, you are a liar and braggart." She turned to Belinda. "Is he really your father?"

"I don't know and I don't care. I've never seen this bear before this week. And I don't want to see him again. Get lost, Polonius! Leave Polar Paradise on the next helicopter. Pay your bill before you go."

THE FLYING TIGERS
WHITE TWIN BENGALS

BENedict   and   **GAL**atea
TIGRIS

Huntley opened the door. The Frau, Colonel and Flying Tigers bared their formidable teeth and the old polar shuffled out followed by the muskrat and her two attendants. Octavius turned to the elk. "Wally, sorry if you expected to sell the ship and the route. Maybe she'll change her mind."

"No thanks, Octavius. The Solar Seas Executive Committee just voted against the sale, Between your properties and facilities and our cruise capabilities, I believe we have a winner without any help from Ms. Muskrat. I personally think she would have destroyed the venture to make a buck. It's still early. Why don't we all have another round of drinks and dinner on Solar Seas Cruise Lines. Invite all your associates. Maybe we can watch the muskrat, gorillas and bears take off for Abeardeen. Speaking of bears, where is that secretary of his? I can't remember a more offensive individual."

Octavius snorted, "As Bel said, "I don't know and I don't care. Good riddance." Little did he know.

That evening, the Octavians and Wally Wapiti gathered together in the Polar Lounge. The elk had developed a taste for Lion and Unicorn's 25 year old vintage scotch served in the castle bar. Fiona promised him a trip on the superyacht down to Baltasound to meet the proprietors of the world's northernmost pub. Chita, Otto and Howard, bowls of champagne in paw were entertaining the Solar Seas CEO. "You're in for a real treat with those two. We'll ask Fiona to get them to do their fighting routine." They looked at the rest of the Octavians who laughed and stood, rapped on the tables and shouted:

> *"The Lion and the Unicorn*
> *Were fighting for the crown.*
> *The Lion beat the Unicorn*
> *All about the town.*
>
> *Some gave them white bread*
> *And some gave them brown;*
> *Some gave them plum cake*
> *And drummed them out of town!"*

The elk laughed. "What does it mean?"

Fiona answered. "Och, Darned if we know. Even those two reprobates don't have a certain answer. We think The Lion and the Unicorn are symbols of the United Kingdom. The lion stands for England and the unicorn for Scotland. The combination dates back to 1603."

"But what about the breads and plum cake?"

"That seems to be a mystery made up to fit the rhyme. You'll get white and brown bread at the pub but we've stopped serving plum cake. Too sticky."

Laughter all around. Wally said, "I can't wait to meet these characters and buy a substantial supply of their whisky."

"We'll see that you have a pure barry time."

"Pure barry?"

"Braw plus."

"Braw plus?"

Chita translated. It means wonderful."

"OK. I'm up for a braw time, especially since we decided not to sell the North Wind or this castle. In the meantime, I'll try another whisky."

More laughter.

The mirth stopped as Polonius shuffled into the lounge looking distraught. "I can't find Paul. I left him in my suite when I came up to yours with Ms. Muskrat. He's not there and he's not in his own room. Do you know where he is? I can't leave here without him. He has all my money and documents. Can you organize a search?"

The Great Bear nodded at the Octavians.

Jaguar Jack got on his phone and Lord David went out into the lobby to summon up his security team. The lounge staff had remembered seeing him earlier. The concierge didn't remember but said, "Sorry, all these polar bears look alike."

Two local constables who were still on site after overseeing the *North Wind's* departure joined in the hunt. The Twins and their Ursulas vigorously set out looking on each floor of the castle. No Luck!

The roar of the giant shuttle chopper's engines echoed up from the heliport. It was carrying, among others, the muskrat and gorillas to Abeardeen. Lord David radioed the chopper. Paul wasn't on it.

They called the yacht. He wasn't among the tourists. The search spread out.

"Call the *North Wind*. Do you think he stowed away?"

Belinda looked at Octavius. "What do you think happened, Tavi? Do you think he just wandered off the property. It's getting darker. I can't stand the bear but I'd hate to think of him falling off a cliff."

"Don't worry, Bel. He'll be found. Alive or Dead!"

Chapter Seven

Harold pulls in a body quite dead.
A drowned polar with wounds near his head.
He gives David a call.
Has he come upon Paul?
Is it some other tourist instead?

Next morning, now that **North Wind** was gone, Harold, the Sea Otter in charge of the resort's water craft and facilities examined the travel center and walkways ensuring everything was ready for the cruise ship's return in a few days. Next he checked out the superyacht **Bel's Barge** for today's excursion. The kitchen and lounge staff would be descending on the boat preparing for the day's outing of mimosas, brunch, deep sea fishing, sightseeing and a stop in Baltasound and Lion and Unicorn's establishment for thirty five eager tourists, all ready to go.

After we returned from Australia and our sail on the Great Barrier Reef, Belinda, with enthusiastic support from the twins, decided to buy a medium sized superyacht not unlike **the Reef Roamer** and base it at Polar Paradise. The twins came up with the name - **Bel's Barge**.

Weather permitting. the boat provides daily excursions for thirty passengers at a time and has become a very popular feature at the resort over a very short time. Brunch, deep sea fishing, sightseeing, snorkeling and ski-dooing all finish up with a stop at Baltasound and the newly refurbished pub and inn run by the inimitable Lion and Unicorn. Their wines and liquors are second to none in Scotland, land of glorious Scotch whiskies.

Occasionally, Marlin, when he is in residence will join with his dolphin pals from his days at the court of the Prince of Whales and provide entertainment by cavorting in the sea around the boat and the snorkelers. A return to his days as Court Jester and Magician. Now, he's a Multiverse scientist.

It's another reason the Solar Seas Cruise Company enthusiastically supports its partnership with Polar Paradise. Another reason why Ellen Muskrat was so eager to buy into the enterprise. It didn't happen.

As Harold skittered along, he thought he saw an object floating a short distance away near the shoreline. Jumping in a small dinghy, he paddled over to the thing intent on removing it before any of the resort guests wandered down to the beach. Everything must be pristine or he'd hear from Ms. Fairbearn or worse yet, the Bearoness.

As he approached the object, he became increasingly aware that this was a large, white-furred body floating face down, shifting in and out with the waves. A drunk who fell into the sea? Off the ship or out of the hotel? He took out his cell phone and placed a call to Lord David who is in charge of the resort's security.

"Lord David. This is Harold. You and your staff better get down to the shoreline near the travel center. I have a polar bear's body floating here. I'm sure he or she is dead. No, I don't know who it is. I don't know whether he or she fell off the ship or was a guest in the hotel. Radio the *North Wind*. See if they're missing a passenger. Check our own guests. I'm towing the body to the shore. Better tell Octavius and the Bearoness. OK! I'll be here. What a mess!"

By the time he made it in with the body in tow, the security team was in place by the shoreline. Two of the large dogs under Lord David's direction pulled the polar's body onto the beach. "It's a male, Lord David, young. Looks like his neck is broken. Do you know who he is?"

"Not definitely but I have a good idea. This could be an accident or a murder. I've called the local police from Baltasound."

Octavius made his way down to the beach along with Belinda, the Frau and Colonel Where. He turned to Lord David. "Have you spoken with the *North Wind*?"

"Yes, everyone is accounted for on the ship."

"So he came from the resort. I think it's Paul. Get Polonius down here to do a positive identification."

"The local police have called Shetland Yard. Superintendent Nigel Wardlaw is on his way up from Lerwick. Your friend, Fetlock Holmes, happens to be in the Shetlands on another case and will be accompanying him. They should be here in a few hours."

"Thanks, David. If it is the secretary, he wasn't very good at making friends and that broken neck looks suspicious. Blunt instrument? Did you find a weapon?"

"No, if there is one, it's probably deep under the waves. Here comes the Senator."

"What's this all about, Doctor Bear? Have your people found Paul?"

"I'm afraid we may have, Polonius. Is this Paul?" He pointed toward the soaking body and its wounds.

"Oh, God! It's him. Who did this? Why? I hold you responsible. You and that ungrateful daughter of mine. I need him. He had my money and documents. My reelection campaign will be a shambles. Somebody is taking it out on me."

Octavius looked skyward and said to himself. "So much for concern over his assistant's death. It's all him, his indictment and his wretched election. That boar is a case of total ego. The Narcissist Polar. They were a matched pair. Well, I'll leave it to the Super and Fetlock to deal with when they arrive.. My sleuthing days are over."

Hardly!

He turned to Jaguar Jack and Dancing Dan. "Will you two please take the Senator inside? Tell Fiona to get him a drink. Cover the body and let's wait for the Medical Examiner to come from Lerwick.. Then one of you take a look at Paul's room but don't touch anything. Let's give the

Superintendent and Fetlock Holmes the benefit of what might be an undisturbed crime scene. Of course, he may have been killed anywhere. Ursula, ask Howard to stop up at the Bearonial Suite. I have an assignment for him. Get Maury, too."

Belinda had been standing by silently shaking her head. She walked over to Harold. "Should we cancel today's yacht excursion?"

The Sea Otter said, "It's a bit late for that, ma'am. Several of the guests have already arrived. I'll tell them it was an accident. It may well be true. If any of them don't want to take the trip, we'll refund their money. Some of the ladies may be upset. We'll see."

She turned to Octavius. 'What's this assignment you have for Howard."

"Join us in the Bearonial Suite and we'll discuss it. Ursula, tell Fiona not to allow Polonius to finish his drink. Give him a new one and hold on to the first bowl. We'll need it. Time for a little DNA profiling."

Belinda smiled, "Aha! I should have thought of that myself. Let's see who this Senator really is or isn't."

On the way back into the lobby, they were intercepted by a tall, slim, middle aged male polar bear. "Excuse me, Bearoness, may I have a moment of your time?"

"I'm sorry, sir. My mate and I are tied up in an important matter at the moment. Perhaps a bit later. I'll have the desk contact you. May I have your name and room number?"

"I'm in room 430 east. My name is Barton Black. I believe I'm your brother."

*****

Shock and dismay. She made an appointment and they headed for the lifts. "Oh dear, Tavi. I'm awash with new found relatives or phonies after my money. Why don't you have this problem?"

"Are you kidding, Bel? I have Agrippa as my real stepbrother. How sleazy can you get? He's been a thorn in my side and my mother's since he was born. Thank goodness he's in jail for a long stretch. That malware exercise on the **Solarwind** sealed his fate for quite a while." *(See Book 18 and 19)*

" I forgot about him."

"I wish I could." They reached the suite doors being held open by their butler. "Here we are and Howard is waiting for us along with the omnipresent Ursula. And here comes Maury with another Ursula. All right, Huntley. It's a bit early for raw champagne but some mimosas will do nicely."

The Husky set off to the kitchen to fetch the drinks trolleys.

They wandered into the large sitting room. Belinda was still shaking her head. 'This is ridiculous. Could that polar really be my brother Barton? I wasn't sure he was still alive. Neither was Aunt Donna. Hello, Howard! Hello Maury."

The porcupine mock-bowed to the Bearoness and Octavius. "Madame and Sir. How can this Erethizontid be of service?"

She laughed again. "You could start by telling me how to pronounce that. Octavius has an assignment for you."

"I live to serve, milady. Octavius?"

"Howard, let's get some use out of that elaborate laboratory you have down in the sub-basement. Can you, Ursula and your devices do DNA profiling?"

Howard Watt PhD

"Haven't had much call for it but yes, we can. Who's the possible culprit?"

"Actually, there are two of them. Polar Bears. One is that pompous Senator Polonius from Alaska. Says he's Belinda's father. We don't believe it. The other just claimed to be Belinda's brother Barton. Fiona, down in the lounge, is getting a half empty drinks bowl from Bel's supposed sire. We'll collect the other sample from the 'brother' when we meet with him later."

The porcupine clacked his jaws and grunted. "It just so happens that I have DNA profiles on all the Octavians including the Bearoness and you. Once I get the Senator's sample extracted, it should be easy to do a comparison. Then I can start to work on the other guy. Hey, this is interesting! I haven't had much chance to do this kind of work. Marlin is going out with his dolphin pals to entertain the yacht goers or he'd join me. Ursula, can you ask Fiona to bring the sample down to the lab. I'll get started right away."

Octavius turned to me. "Maury, See what you and Ursula can find out about this Barton Black. There are too many coincidences popping up here, including the death of Polonius' secretary, Paul. I hate coincidences."

"You think there's a connection?"

"Between what and what? I don't know but I don't like it. See what you can do."

"Suppose there is a relationship?"

"I guess we'll have to deal with it but I'm betting Polonius is a Class A fraud trying to manipulate funds for his legal defense and reelection, assuming he's a Senator at all."

"Didn't your Alaskan friends and relatives give you a description that pretty much matches this guy? Limp, wound, scar?"

Belinda snarled. "Yes, they did. I don't really care if he's a Senator and I care even less if he's my father. I just want to expose him for the money grubbing wretch he is and get him shipped out of here."

"Not before the police have a shot at him, Bel. He could be Paul's murderer if it was murder. For that matter, it could be this Barton Black, whoever he is. And there's Ellen Muskrat's gorillas. They're strong enough to break a polar's neck. I asked the police at Abeardeen to impound her jet so they can't leave the country. And there could be another culprit among all the resort guests. Too many suspects."

"It could have been an accident ."

"Yes, I know. Superintendent Wardlaw and Fetlock Holmes should be here in an hour or so with a Medical Examiner. When they arrive, Maury, round up Lord David, Chita, Otto, the Frau and Colonel and join Belinda and me in the large conference room. Meanwhile I'm going to have another chat with the Senator."

Bel frowned. "You'll forgive me if I don't come with you. Just the sight of him raises my hackles."

"OK. Keep that neck fur under control. And Howard, keep us posted."

"You betcha! Heigh-ho, heigh-ho. Down to the lab I go! Let's see what I remember! I'll still have to hit the manual but fortunately, our equipment and Ursula are artificially intelligent. Onward!"

He trotted out of the apartment, heading for the elevator and sub-basement laboratories. The place was a scientific wonderland. Magical! He and Marlin were the wizards. There were four separate rooms. The seldom used DNA Analysis lab; the general purpose physics, biology and chemistry workrooms; the AI computer center primarily used by the twins for their games and research and the Multiverse Interplanetary search, navigation and launch site where he and Marlin spent most of their time. When the Octavians journeyed to the outer cosmos and the many exoplanets circling distant stars, they took off from this center or a twin facility back in Cincinnati at the Bear's Lair. Both buildings were equipped with strong radio telescopes, GPS receivers and Multiverse launch, tracking and recovery equipment.

The Advanced Super Computing Center at the Deep Data Hexagon in Kentucky, home of Chief Technical Officer L. Condor, senior scientist Byzantia Bonobo and a large staff of computer and information developers and scientists, sported the very latest in equipment and software. It is here that the Ursulas are developed and supported.

On the other side of the floor in the hotel's sub-basement was a medical facility staffed by a full time nurse practitioner. The tourist population suffered accidents and health incidents with great regularity. An adjacent room served as a morgue. Animals died at resorts like everywhere else, including ships. Right now, Paul's body had just been transferred there awaiting the Shetland Yard Medical Examiner who was flying up with Superintendent Laidlaw and Fetlock Holmes.

Howard went into the DNA Analysis Lab, flipped switches, booted up software, analytic tools and databases. He waited for Fiona to arrive with the samples from Polonius Black. A knock on the door and she entered, carrying a drinks bowl and a handkerchief.

She handed them carefully to the porcupine.

"Here you are, Doctor Watt. Fresh from the Polar Lounge. Not sure how she did it but Molly, or was it Dolly, managed to clip some fur from the Senator in addition to rescuing his half finished drink. Is that all you need? If so, I'll let you do your magic. This place always amazes me. You really know how to manage these things? What does his drink and fur have to do with anythin'?"

"Thanks, Fiona! Yes, I do know how to run this equipment. His saliva and hair will tell us quite a lot. Now let's see if the Senator is the Bearoness' father. I have my doubts. Want to take bets?"

"No thanks! I only wager on sure things."

"So you're convinced he's a phony?"

"Och, fer sure! So was that secretary of his. We Dandie Dinmonts can sniff a bad 'un out a mile away. We're terriers, after all, descended from hunters and game dogs. I like bears. Otherwise, I wouldna take this job. The Bearoness and the Doctor are grand. So are their twins. But those two Alaskan bears had 'eas-onarach' written all over them."

"eas-onarach?"

"You know. It's Scots-Gaelic. What's your word-Dishonest?"

"Got it in one. Ya smart boots. Dishonest! They're crooked as they come. Will your fancy equipment tell yer that?"

"Not directly but it will tell us whether he's related to Bearoness Belinda. Through a process called DNA Profiling. We examine his genome and do comparisons. Would you like yours examined?'

"Doctor Watt! I may be a former barmaid but I'm a good girl and nobody is going to examine any genome thingy of mine even if you are a scientist, What is it anyway?"

The Development of Civilization Volume 20

Part 4

Genomics and DNA Profiling

From "An Introduction to Faunapology"
by Octavius Bear Ph.D.
Thanks to Wikipedia

In the fields of molecular biology and genetics, a genome is defined as all the genetic information of an organism. The study of the genome is called genomics. The genomes of many organisms have been sequenced and various regions have been annotated. The definition of 'genome' that's commonly used in the scientific literature is usually restricted to the large chromosomal DNA molecules in bacteria.

DNA profiling (also called DNA fingerprinting and genetic fingerprinting) is the process of determining an individual's characteristics. It is a forensic technique in criminal investigations, comparing criminal suspects' profiles to DNA evidence to assess the likelihood of their involvement in a crime. It is also used in paternity testing; to establish immigration eligibility; and in genealogical and medical research.

Starting in the 1980s, scientific advances allowed the use of DNA as a material for the identification of an individual. Although 99.9% of animal DNA sequences are the same in every individual, enough of the DNA is different to distinguish one individual from another, unless they are identical twins. A process for DNA profiling in 1984 led to the first use of DNA profiling in a criminal case and has since become more universally accepted due to improved techniques.

When a sample such as blood, hair or saliva is obtained, the DNA is only a small part of what is present in the sample. Before the DNA can be analyzed, it must be extracted from the cells and purified. Once the DNA is free, it can be separated from all other cellular components.

A careful series of comparisons follow and similarities established.

It is possible to use DNA profiling as evidence of genetic relationship although such evidence varies in strength from weak to positive. However, testing that shows no relationship is absolutely certain. Now, what about our subjects and our suspicions? In this case we're looking for negatives.

We plan to use this technique to determine Polonius Polar and Barton Black's relationship, if any, to **Bearoness Belinda Béarnaise Bruin Bear (nee Black)**.We'll see what Howard comes up with. Stay tuned!

Chapter Eight

Who is Barton? We all want to know.
Is Polonius' claim really so?
Let's compare DNA.
What does profiling say?
Are they Belinda's kin? Yes or No?

While Howard went to the lab, I set off in search of this Barton character and Octavius headed down to the lounge to face off against the so-called Senator.

On his way into the salon, he passed Fiona carrying a half empty drinks bowl and a white handkerchief. She winked at the great Bear and said. "I don't know how she did it but Dolly not only managed to switch his drinks but she got a sample of his fur. I'm on my way down to the lab and Dr. Watt. He's cute for a porcupine."

Octavius winked back, spotted Polonius, asked Polly for a bowl of Lion and Unicorn's best Scotch and drifted toward the old polar. Before he could reach his target he was set upon by two brown and white whirlwinds, each with a soda and an Ursula laptop strapped around their necks.

"Hi Dad! We've been looking for you. We're working on our new game. ***Bears Up North!*** We heard a polar bear got killed. Can we use him in our plot? Who is he? Why is he dead? Who did it?"

"Short answer: We don't know. Shorter answer. No you can't. The police are on their way and I don't want you interfering with their work."

"Maybe later after they find the killer?"

"We're not even sure there is a killer. It may have been an accident."

"Aw, gee. That's no fun."

"Go work on something else."

"Awwww!

While this exchange was going on, Octavius had sidled nearer and nearer to Polonius' table. The old Polar gestured. "Doctor Bear, please join me. Are those two hyperactive teen-agers related to you?"

"Yes, they're mine and they're your grandchildren, if your claim to being Belinda's father is true."

The old bear choked on his drink and stuttered. "Why, yes! I suppose so. It hadn't occurred to me. Indeed."

"Come now, Polonius. How long are you going to keep up this charade."

"What are you talking about? What charade? I am Belinda's father. I did promise Ms. Muskrat I would urge my daughter to sell this monstrous castle. It was in Belinda's best interest. Ellen Muskrat was prepared to be quite generous to her."

"And to you."

A pause. "Well, yes. Ms. Muskrat was inclined to reward me for my efforts."

"Which reward would support your Political Action Committee. To say nothing of your legal fees for fighting your possible indictment for fraud and deceptive senatorial testimony."

"What? Where did you hear that? Sheer nonsense! No such thing!"

Octavius shrugged and wondered how Howard was doing with his tests.

"Change of subject, Doctor Bear. What news of Paul's death? That event has shaken my world. Unless I can gain access to his room and find my money and credit cards, I'll be unable to pay your outrageous bills that Belinda insists I handle."

"No, our fees are not outrageous. Just ask the flood of other tourists how they feel and both Belinda and I insist that you pay. The police from Shetland Yard are coming shortly to investigate the death. I'm sure they'll let you in his room after they're finished. And while the local constabulary is also here, I'd be happy to turn you over to them for non-payment."

"What, sir! I'm a United States Senator."

"Perhaps, perhaps. Please make yourself available for Superintendent Nigel Wardlaw and Mr. Fetlock Holmes."

"The famous detective Fetlock Holmes? Why is he involved?"

"He is a long standing associate of mine in dealing with many of the crimes and criminals I have pursued and he has worked many cases with the Superintendent here in the UK. Excuse me! I must leave."

He finished his Scotch and headed out of the lounge to a goods lift that stopped at the laboratory sub-basement and Howard Watt.

*****

Meanwhile, I had discovered Barton Black standing on the travel center walkway watching the superyacht *Bel's Barge*, leaving for the day's excursion.

"Not interested in deep sea fishing, Mr. Black?

"Not today, thanks. You have the advantage over me, sir. Who are you?"

"Mauritius Meerkat! Maury to friends and acquaintances. I am Octavius Bear's faithful associate as well as assistant to the Bearoness and their twins. I understand you claim to be Belinda's brother."

"I believe I am and anxious to prove it."

"Well, we'd like to assist you in reaching that goal."

"How?"

"Are you willing to undergo DNA profiling? All it takes is a swab in your mouth or a squib of your hair and our lab equipment does the rest. We have the Bearoness' profile in our database. We'll compare the two and see what we can see."

"I've heard of that. You have a lab here?"

"Down in a hidden sub-basement, we have a technological wonderland. I can't give you access but take my word for it. It's awesome. Octavius Bear is a scientific genius and we have several members on our staff who are world class practitioners."

"OK, I'm game. What about that phony Senator who's claiming to be Belinda's and my father?"

"Oh, we have him covered. Only he doesn't know it. Not yet!"

"Anything that sinks his ship is fine with me. Some father! He's a self-aggrandizing blowhard. And his secretary's a real jerk. Sorry our Mom is dead but I'd like to get to know Belinda."

(And maybe get your paws on some of her money. Oh well, I'll give him the benefit of the doubt.)

"Meanwhile, tell me about yourself."

"I'm a salesbear for a technical consulting firm. I live in New Jersey. Right near the Liberty Cruise Ship port. Solar Seas was making a big deal over their new Arctic service and mentioned Belinda's resort in their news releases. I decided to sign on and check if she was my sister. Little did I know that my so-called father would be here as well. I'm sure he's a fraud."

"But you're not."

"No! Let's get this DNA test going. That should prove I'm not lying."

"That would be refreshing. We've already had our fill of lies."

"Well, after we've proven I am who I say I am, I'd like to have a chat with Belinda.'

"Would that chat include a discussion about money?"

"Yes! I'll be honest. I don't make that much in sales and would be most grateful for any help she'd be willing to extend."

Suddenly the sound of a tactical helicopter buzzed over the shore line and turned toward the heliport. The words HM Police were emblazoned on the fuselage. The cavalry was arriving. I looked at Barton and pointed toward the sky. "All right! Duty calls. I have to meet that chopper. Why don't you wait in your room and we'll give you a buzz when we're ready."

Barton looked up as the whirlybird floated in for a landing. "Ah ha! Calling in Shetland Yard. Do you think that miserable personal secretary was murdered?"

"Don't know. That's what we intend to find out and catch the perp if it's ursinocide. See you later."

I walked over to the expanded heliport and the now-landed police chopper. A rear cargo door of the ship opened and a bearded collie stepped out onto the tarmac followed by a clearly uncomfortable black horse taking the steps with difficulty. A uniformed sergeant and black clad ferret joined them.

Octavius had come back from the lab when he had heard the helicopter had arrived. He came out the door of the castle, crossed the drawbridge and trotted up, paw extended to greet the passengers. Lord David, Dancing Dan and Jaguar Jack appeared from the Security office. Our contingent was completed by the arrival of Harold and the Wolves. *(and of course, Ursula in her laptop and me.)*

Octavius smiled, "Gentlebeasts of the law! Welcome!"

The uniformed sergeant and Medical Examiner stepped forward and joined the pair. Paw and hoof shakes all around. Fetlock Holmes nodded his stately head. "Greetings Octavius. I understand another murder has been committed. This castle seems to attract violence."

Superintendent Nigel Wardlaw and   **Fetlock Holmes**

Fortunately, the Twins weren't there to hear that remark. They would have immediately added it to the script of their newest electronic game **Bears Up North**. But Fetlock Holmes was right. Polar Paradise has been the scene of several aggressive deaths and near deaths in the past. We weren't yet sure whether this one was deliberate or an accident.

The Great Bear corrected the horse. "We don't know for certain if it is murder." He turned to the medical Examiner. "I hope you can shed some light on the subject, Doctor." The ferret nodded his head. "Where's the body?"

"In our morgue. Jack, can you take him down there? We found him floating down at the shore."

The jaguar patted the examiner on his head, much to the ferret's annoyance. "Follow me, amigo."

Superintendent Wardlaw asked. "Who's the body?"

I answered. "A polar bear. Paul by name. He was the personal secretary to Senator Polonius Polar Black of Alaska who claims he is the Bearoness' father. Two extremely annoying individuals. Not annoying enough to justify killing if the Examiner says it's murder but he certainly had a talent for making enemies. That includes Ellen Muskrat and her two gorilla bodyguards. I understand you have them detained in Abeardeen."

Wardlaw turned to Octavius. "Yes, and she's damned unhappy about it. Her lawyers are raising hell with the Commissioner. We need to either clear them or arrest them in record time. We're holding them on your say-so and that is only going to work for a little longer."

"Well then. Let's get cracking. This is Harold Otter. He found the corpse floating in the bay. He was preparing our superyacht for the day's fishing and exploring excursion when he spotted it."

"Did you see anybody or anything suspicious, Harold?"

"No sir. I saw something floating near the shore. Thought it was some kind of flotsam or jetsam tossed from the *North Wind* cruise ship when she was leaving. Until I got closer. That's when I called security. They rang the police who called you. Can I go now? I've got this excursion to get under way."

Fetlock nodded. "Go to it! Gentlebeasts, let's look at his room. Wait, who's this coming over?"

A large polar senior citizen approached. He recognized the celebrated horse, ignoring the rest of the party including Octavius and Super Wardlaw. In his best 'I'm very important' tone he addressed the detective. "Mr. Fetlock Holmes, I am aware of your famous self. I'm Polonius Polar Black, Senior Senator from the great American state of Alaska. Perhaps you have heard of me. I assume it is the death of my aide, Paul Polar that brings you to this castle. I am here to assist you in your inquiries. Paul was a highly efficient and capable secretary. I shall miss his assistance."

"Thank you Senator, but you should be addressing your offer to Superintendent Nigel Wardlaw of Shetland Yard and Sergeant Byrne. It is their investigation. I am here entirely in a consulting capacity."

Polonius looked askance at the two lawmen and granted them both a gratuitous nod, once again ignoring The Great Bear or the rest of us Octavians.

The Border Collie returned his nod and said, "After we register, we will take a look at your secretary's room, Senator. Please accompany us.

But first we need to hear the Medical Examiner's conclusions. Here he comes. Accident or Murder, Doctor?"

Jaguar Jack and the ferret were returning from the morgue. Two members of the castle's security staff were behind them pushing a gurney with the victim's body on it. The Medical Examiner turned to them. "Load it on the copter, lads. I'll take it back to Lerwick with me and perform a more detailed autopsy. Superintendent, I assume you and Mister Holmes will be staying on. I think you'll want to. This was a murder."

Wardlaw shook his head. "I assumed as much, Doctor. How did you reach that conclusion?"

"He did not drown. Broken neck induced by a large blunt object. Some random bruises probably from the sea bottom but there are claw marks on his forearms, shoulders and head. Possibly a fight. Look for someone else equipped with claws sporting a few bruises and wounds."

The Super replied, "Thank you, Doctor. We'll proceed by treating this as an ursinocide by animal or animals unknown. There will, no doubt, be a coroner's inquest, Octavius, can the resort accommodate the three of us here for the next day or so and provide a conference room?"

The Great Bear turned to me and said, "Please see to it." I nodded in reply and called over Ms. Fairbearn to get things in motion. Polonius trailed along behind.

Belinda had entered the lobby, greeted the policemen and detective and listened as Octavius brought her up to speed.

Polonius was wringing his paws. "I can't believe it. Paul could be abrasive at times but who would want to kill him and why?"

The Great Bear said, "We intend to find out, Senator. I'm sure the police will have more questions for you. They'll be heading down to Paul's room shortly. Please join them. They'll meet you in the lobby."

The Polar shuffled off.

Octavius snorted, "I'll be glad to see the last of him." Belinda replied, "You and me both. You know, I never really cared before but now I wonder who and where my real father is. This guy is certainly not."

Chapter Nine

His DNA profile is in
And the Senator's guilty as sin.
It's what we always knew.
He's a faker, it's true.
Let the great revelation begin!

Chuckling to himself. Howard came up from the sub-basement lab and took the lift up to the Bearonial Suite. He had called ahead and the Wolves, Huntley, Chita and I were already there. Belinda had just returned. She asked Ursula to call Octavius. It took a few minutes for the Great Bear to disentangle himself from the police after seeing them registered and leading them to their conference/work area. As usual, because of his size, he had to use the goods lift *(freight elevator)* to get to the Bearonial Suite. And, as usual, his nine foot, 1400 pound frame attracted curiosity. Polar bears believed they were the largest ursines. Octavius proved otherwise. On the other hand, Polars far outnumbered Kodiaks.

Howard arrived simultaneously with Octavius. We all looked at him expectantly. Chita blurted, "Well, Spiny, what's the verdict?'

He looked at the Bearoness. "I ran the process twice with two different samples, using saliva and fur, just to be sure. Ursula will validate it. If you two were any further apart in DNA makeup, we'd have to change the laws of biology."

Belinda smiled, "As I expected. No match?"

"Not even close. In spite of his claims, Polonius Polar is not your father. I doubt he's even a Black."

"Well, I'm going to face him down."

Octavius snorted. "Not so fast, Bel.' He looked around. "Let's all keep this information to ourselves for the moment. The Medical Examiner pronounced Paul's death a murder. There may be no connection but I think our friendly Senator may be playing fast and loose with the truth in several instances. You've already refused to acknowledge his paternity and he doesn't know we took his DNA profile to prove he's a fake. Let's hold on to our proof and use it if and when we need it."

"Who knows what Ellen Muskrat may have come up with although I'm sure she's seen through Polonius by now. She just wants to get back to Atlanta ASAP. Those gorillas of hers are more than capable of killing off Paul. Wardlaw wants to keep them in Scotland for the duration."

He scanned the room. "Any objections?"

Silence! Then I asked. 'What about this Barton character who claims to be your brother. He's not that crazy about Polonius or Paul. He's more than willing to be profiled. Are you interested?"

Belinda and Octavius answered together. "Let's do it! Maury and Howard, get his samples down to the lab. Don't say anything to Barton about our results with Polonius."

"I mentioned we were planning to do the Senator's profile."

"Well, we haven't done it yet. OK?"

"Gotcha! Back to the lab, Howard. I'll scare up our test subject and then join the yacht."

Octavius said, "I'm going to rejoin the detectives. Next stop is Paul's room. Polonius will be with us to cast any light on the state of the location and point out any clues. We can watch him. Of course, we're not sure where Paul was killed or exactly how. The Medico says blunt instrument and choking."

*****

The consulting horse detective asked, "How long has Paul been with you, Senator?"

"Seven years, Mr. Holmes. He joined my last election campaign. As you may know, we senators serve for six years and I'm about to seek reelection. I have a staff back at my headquarters in Juneau but Paul was my traveling aide-de-camp, so to speak. I shall have to find a replacement quickly."

'Forgive my asking but there seems to be a bit of scandal attached to your tenure. Something to do with lawsuits over falsification of documentation and testimony?"

"Lies created by my political opponents. I plan a vigorous defense."

"Which will require a major expense. Were you expecting Doctor Bear, the Bearoness or Ms. Ellen Muskrat to provide the wherewithal?"

"Those options seem to have disappeared. I'll have to seek help elsewhere."

"Was Paul involved in trying to raise those monies?"

"Yes, of course. It was part of his job to raise cash for my activities. Him and my PACs."

"PAC?"

"Political Action Committee. In the United States, a political action committee is an organization that pools contributions from members and donates those funds to campaigns for or against candidates, ballot initiatives, or legislation. I rely on several PACs to support my work as a Senator and my bids for reelection."

"We have similar organizations in the UK with different names and probably different rules."

"I suppose so. I was counting on a healthy donation from Ms. Muskrat and one from my daughter."

"Your daughter?"

"The Bearoness is my daughter although she won't admit to it."

"Why is that?"

"She is a willful royalist. No respect for the democratic process."

"But wasn't she born and raised in the United States? When did you see her last?"

The Senator blanched and turned away. They proceeded down the corridor.

"Let's see what there is to be seen." Superintendent Wardlaw thanked Ms. Fairbearn for opening the door to Paul's room. The space was not spacious. The manager had made good on her threat to park the smart aleck in a small and nondescript part of the resort- the low rent district. .

There was precious little to indicate the room had even been occupied. The bed was made, the small bathroom held only hotel toiletries that looked unused. There were two small valises in the closet. The sergeant twiddled with the locks and got them open. Paul had used the same combination on both. One case was filled with personal items, a couple of notebooks and a slim laptop. No cell phone. The other case held wallets filled with American and British currencies. "Hmm, was our victim a pickpocket?"

It looked that way!

*****

Next morning and another yacht excursion was prepping. No mention of Paul's death. I brought Barton into a small conference room where Howard was waiting. Introductions and on to a quick description of the profiling and comparison processes. Howard flashed his prickly smile and said, "I understand you work in technical sales so this shouldn't be totally mysterious to you."

"Yeah, I've read some of the material on genetics and ancestry."

"Fine! We'll soon see. Unfortunately, there are some other scientific apparatus and equipment in the lab that are top secret so I can't invite you to join me down there. I want to use two different DNA sources for the test. Your saliva and a strand of your fur. Our extraction and profiling gear is highly sophisticated, accurate and discriminating. We extract your DNA, map it and compare it against a database of profiles. The Bearoness is on file and we'll see how close you two stack up, if at all. If there's no match or very little, that's the end of our discussion. If it's identical, you're probably twins. If it's somewhere in between, we'll need to see how convincing you are by delving into your history. Now, are you willing to let us do these tests?"

'You bet. I'm convinced I'm her brother."

"OK, I have this swab to gather a saliva sample and I'm going to cut off a length of your fur. Then I'll go down to the lab. It'll take about an hour. You can stay here, go out to the lounge or the theatre or down to the shore. I'll have you paged."

I piped up. "Howard, Barton. I'm due to join the revelers on the yacht in just a few minutes. Do you have any more need for my presence?"

The porcupine shook his head, "Nope, Maury. Thanks for your help."

Barton looked at the two of us. "Probably none of my business but I got the impression that you ran the same tests on my supposed father. The Great Senator from the Great State of Alaska."

"Not yet! We plan to." *(A lie but a necessary lie. Polonius had failed dramatically but we wanted to keep that a secret.)*

We started out of the room heading our separate ways.

I bowed. "Well, gentlebeasts. I'm off to sail the briny. Barton, why don't you sign up for an excursion. They're lots of fun. You might catch a fish or two and the Lion and Unicorn Pub is a real hoot. Who knows? You might meet an interesting she-bear. See you later."

I skittered off to the jetty.

I thought I heard Howard humming to himself. I wasn't sure where Barton was off to. Suppose he really is Belinda's brother? I wondered.

Chapter Ten

On the superyacht out in the bay,
With the tourists all busy at play.
The excursion is bound
To approach Baltasound
And a pub to round out their fun day.

"Sailing, sailing over the bounding main!" A female arctic fox who had visited and revisited the mimosa pitchers and drinks trolleys with intense passion was standing somewhat unsteadily on the prow of *Bel's Barge,* singing enthusiastically off key. She was watching Marlin and his dolphin confreres from the court of the Prince of Whales going through their repertoire of synchronized leaps, dives and high speed maneuvers to the delight of the day-long excursionists. The penguin passengers were leaping off the stern platform and chasing around after the dolphins. I was on the bridge with Harold and Otto.

Two of the lounge waitresses, Molly and Holly, had served a late morning brunch and mimosas prior to an hour or so of deep sea fishing for non-sentient aquatic vertebrates. The polar bears had to be restrained from jumping in the bay and chasing their prey. Then after cruising along the coastline and taking in the cliffs, beaches, dunes and occasional seals sunning themselves on the rocks, the superyacht cruised up to the Baltasound jetty where each day the locals were prepared to welcome the tourists *(and their money.)*

We docked and the passengers strode, crawled, staggered and hopped off the boat and strolled along the cobbled street leading to the village center.

Baltasound village was a bit more than a mile square; mostly waterfront with a few fishing boats and other small craft tied up. A ferry slip, about to be occupied by *Bel's Barge*, dominated a short breakwater and pier. A wee kirk and a scattering of cottages, shops and homes made up the remainder of the community. The nearest school is on the outskirts. A small airstrip rounded out the civic features.

A few off-road vehicles were distributed around the streets. At the "four corners" of the village sat the police station, post office and town hall all in one thatched roof building. A petrol station was opposite. A general store occupied third base and home plate was our destination. A great stone pile two stories high with sizeable windows and blue and white shutters. It was actually three connected buildings all under a layer of thatch. It looked like the combined willpower of the occupants was the only thing keeping the roof from sagging to street level.

Movie producers around the world would kill to capture the unself-conscious authenticity of the little town. Chita had produced several short promotional films that appeared on social media and TV channels. I remember the crews crawling all over taking shots of the cottages, cemeteries, kirk, shoppes, the locals and of course, the watering hole. A large, ornate, three dimensional sign mounted on a free-standing pole proclaimed that indeed, we had reached The Lion and the Unicorn. The sign's heraldry was straight out of 'Tales of the Noble Highlanders' and the two sculpted animals, rearing erect, no doubt recently repainted, faced off against each other across an elaborate shield capped off with a crown.

No doubt this was the place. We all approached the doors.

LION AND UNICORN INN AND PUB

My vexillary skills are vry limited but I think I was looking at a reproduction of the Great Seal of Scotland. Another sign filled the windows showing the owners in profile gazing at a barrel of 'spiritus frumenti'. No question!

Suddenly, there was a roar from within the pub and the door slammed open, followed by two North Sea seals barreling out as fast as they could.

"And don't come back in here with that balancin' ball act again. Ye broke half ma glassware, ye twits." This came, no doubt, from the bartender or proprietor who was gifted with a very impressive and stentorian voice. The two seals, rolling over and over hysterically, barking and guffawing, waddled down to the dock, pushing and tossing a ball between them.

"Those two are the village clowns." said Harold. Then winking at Otto. "We have a few otters who also supply some merriment."

"Add a few more to the crowd," I mumbled, as we went through the door into a large, noisy and smoky room that stretched through two of the three connected buildings. The other section may have been a kitchen or a 'ladies lounge.' There were stairs going to the second floor – transient rooms possibly. The walls were festooned with Union Jacks, St. Andrew's Cross flags and a large number of regimental drums. Standing behind the ale and beer taps below a full-size portrait of the Prince of Whales was a real live, honest to God unicorn *(or a horse doing a hell of a makeup job)* and a bit further down the bar, putting a stack of glassware back on the mirrored shelves, was a very regal and currently very annoyed lion.

We moved over to the bar and Harold did the introductions of our tour party and re-introductions of the Polar Paradise denizens. It seems the unicorn was called Unicorn and oddly enough the lion, who had come over to us while wiping his paws on a bar rag, was called Lion. They welcomed Harold who was, no doubt, a regular.

Wally Wapiti sidled up to a stool, sat and looked at Lion. The cat stared back with his large amber eyes. The elk spoke. "Hello, Mr. Lion. I'm Wally Wapiti, president and CEO of the Solar Seas Cruise Line Company. Our ship, **The North Wind,** is part of a new Arctic cruise venture making stops in the North Sea and here in Unst Island at Polar Paradise. We'll be bringing 200 or so passengers to the area every month and we'll make sure they visit Baltasound and your unique establishment. That may have a positive effect on your business. I understand you keep some of the finest Scotch whisky in the country."

Unicorn, who was listening to all of this chipped in, "Nae, finest in the world. By the way, we spell it without the 'e.'" He looked at Lion, "How aboot a welcoming dram of the fifty year old single malt for our new friend, Mr. Wapiti?"

The Lion turned and went into a room behind the bar where we heard the tinkling sounds of bottles and bowls being moved about. He came back out holding a dust covered flagon in his paws. He blew on it revealing that lions have serious bad breath problems.

He had a little trouble uncorking the bottle and I was afraid he was simply going to smash the neck on the bar. The cork finally gave and he poured a healthy swig into a bowl for the elk and one for me. "Gude to see you again, Mr. Mere Cat. Try a few fingers of Old Alicorn." Scotch is not my favorite quaff. I'm a fan of fermented coconut milk VSOP but I lapped at the whisky. Very nice. Otto had no trouble getting a kelp juice and vodka since there was a fair sized otter population among the inn's clientele.

"Yer gude health, Mr. Wapiti and gude cess to your ship."

Wally saluted. "Tell us about this inn." He beckoned Harriet Hare over and asked her to take notes. The columnist turned on her recorder.

"Weeell, we've been in business for over thirty years, Unicorn and me. All of the locals love us *(except for those pesky seals.)* We expanded our lodgings for the workers who were buildin' the travel center up at the castle and we've been getting some tourists looking for some moderate priced fun in the ocean and hiking, don't cha know. Of course, we're renowned for the famous fight we stage. Have ye never heard the old nursery rhyme? It's been around for hundreds of years."

"I was treated to a performance the other night at the Polar Paradise. Your lounge manager Fiona led the customers in the recitation."

"Aye, that Fiona is a bonnie little doggie. Lots of brains and talent. She started as a waitress. She's our enterprise manager now."

"So this fight between the two of you. Who won?"

"I did," they both said.

"What does it mean?"

"Damned if we know. Some smart boots around here think it has to do with Scotland and England comin' together but we were nae part of that parade."

"So you re-enact the fight for the tourists?"

"Complete with everyone drummin.' On special occasions, like our birthdays and such. It always comes out in a tie and we provide ale and whisky and mead along with the brown and white bread. We dinna hae any plum cake anymore. Too gooey."

I asked. "Do you still make mead?"

"Aye, the finest in the kingdom – the world even."

"Well, you know I work for Octavius Bear who is absolutely the world's greatest connoisseur of mead. He makes it himself back in the States."

"Aye, we remember Doctor Bear. Big, tall Kodiak. Loves mead. Sorry he's not with you."

"He's busy right now back at the castle. There's been a death." They gaped.

Some of the passengers had not heard of the floating body before they boarded the yacht. They crowded over to the bar. One of the snow leopards said, "So that's what the police are doing up at the castle. What happened."

Harold briefly described his discovery.

A female caribou rumbled. "Oh dear. Was it murder? Are we all going to be killed in our beds?"

Harold, Otto and I rushed to calm the skittish caribou, reindeer, foxes and musk oxen. The penguin family flapped their flippers and waddled aimlessly about. We finally got them all reassured. The polar bears were not pleased that the victim was one of their species but confident of their weight, size and ferocity, they could not imagine someone doing them in. Unless…suppose the killer was one of their own?

Lion and Unicorn, both inured to deaths, set to serving up their wares, telling tales of Baltasound and Unst and jollying the group with a foreshortened version of their fight minus the brown and white bread. Harriet Hare had been recording all this and was pulling together a feature story minus the murder. She had seen Ellen Muskrat with her gorillas leaving the evening before in a snit. Very few people have thwarted the zillionaire. The sales didn't go through and she wouldn't want to be in Polonius Polar's position right now. She wondered who did Paul Polar in and why. Anyhow, Chita still owed her a dinner. She heard the Castle's chef, Mrs. McRadish was a wizard, even with rabbit food.

The day progressed. After a stay at the Pub and a short tour around the village, the tired and well lubricated tourists straggled back to the superyacht, carrying souvenir bottles of rum, Scotch and grog and pieces of local woodcraft and sewing products. They were ready to return to Polar Paradise. As the boat pulled away from the slip, an off key voice was heard leading the group in "Sailing, sailing, over the bounding main; For many a stormy wind shall blow, ere Jack comes home again!"

Back at the resort, the staff was preparing for another busy evening. In the ballroom, tables were being set up and the dance floor cleaned and polished. The house band would be coming down after playing for the early musical review in the theatre. Another team was supplying music for the Aquabear show. The casino was open and the sounds of fruit *(slot)* machines, laughter and groans filled the air.

Madame Giselle and Otto had the evening off and had joined the other Octavians in the Bearonial Suite where Huntley and one of the Dolly-Holly-Molly-Polly's were serving nibbles and cocktails. I skittered through the lobby and on to the lift heading for the top floor.

I wondered how Barton's DNA tests turned out. I'll have to track Howard down. How will the Bearoness react? How, how, how? And what about Polonius? We'll have to get Ursula to do a check on both of them. Scouring the profundities of Deep Data in search of meaningful information. She does it so well.

Chapter Eleven

After profiling their DNA
What did Howard's analysis say?
Did the two of them win?
Barton's Belinda's twin!
But Polonius' claim? There's no way!

I arrived at the Bearonial Suite just in time to hear the tail end of a conversation among the Octavians. They had been actively discussing the implications of Howard's discovery. ***Belinda and Barton were twins!*** No question about it. He'd run the tests and matches several times. The profiles were identical in all respects except for gender. On the other hand, as they now all knew, Polonius was unrelated, Certainly not Bel's father.

The porcupine had passed this information on to Ursula who in turn passed it on to the Bearoness and Octavius. She was mildly shocked but agreed that Barton had to be told. To be certain, they needed to contact Donna again on Zoom. Her aunt had raised Barton for a short while along with Belinda before he did his disappearing act. If, in addition to the DNA evidence, he could accurately recall his cubhood, Belinda would be convinced.

Octavius was somewhat amused. Belinda's 'father' was a fraud but her 'brother' was the real thing. A twin, no less. Wait till Donna, Wallingford and Juno got the news. They had been certain Polonius was a general purpose phony. The population of Alaska was coming to the same conclusion. The next election may already be settled.

When he heard the news, Barton was not taken aback. It was what he had anticipated although he hadn't expected the relationship to his sister to be that close. He stayed in the lounge, downing Martinis and chatting with Howard about genetics, science and technology. He would wait to be invited in by the Bearoness. Howard left and went up to the Bearonial Suite. "Hang in there, Barton."

Belinda was sitting among the Octavians sipping a bowl of champagne when Howard walked in. "Ah, Howard. Just the porcupine I wanted to see. I got your message from Ursula. How confident are you that he's my twin?"

"Belinda, I checked and rechecked the equipment. Made sure the samples weren't compromised and performed the tests several times each – saliva and fur. I went back and reviewed your profile. It's recent and it was double processed when we took it. I wanted to make sure we had an accurate picture of you and Octavius. Nothing is absolutely certain but I and the DNA process say at 99.999% confidence that you two are twins. By the way, I have equal confidence that you and Polonius are not related. When are you going to tell him?"

"He can wait. Right now, I want to run an unscientific test with my presumed twin. Bring him up here, please. Ursula, see if you can contact Aunt Donna. I want her to quiz Barton."

Just as Howard returned with Barton in tow, Ursula was establishing a Zoom session with Bel's aunt. The Octavians waved at him. He waved back and smiled.

Belinda stared at him. "Hello Barton. I'm told we are related. Interesting, if true. Howard has a high level of certainty that we are twins. I'm willing to accept that if you will have a satisfactory Zoom interview with my Aunt Bella Donna Black. She remembers you. Do you remember her>"

"Aunt Donna? Vaguely. I was just a cub. But sure, let's do it."

"Why don't you go into that anteroom over there away from all of us. Ursula will hook the two of you up and you can chat."

He went into the room and shut the door behind him. He looked at the polar sow on the screen and said, "Hello Aunt Donna, Long time, no see. What can I tell you?"

"Hello Barton! You certainly look like Belinda. OK, you had a tricycle. Do you remember the color and the name you gave it?"

"Let's see. It was blue and white and I called it Woosh."

"Good, now, when was the first time we went fishing? Did you catch anything?"

And so it went.

*****

Down in the conference room assigned to them, the detectives were making notes and questioning members of the staff, Sergeant Byrne was sorting through the contents of Paul's briefcase, taking pictures of the wallets and purses as evidence and preparing to return them to their rightful owners.

Superintendent Wardlaw had just dismissed one of the security staff and was waiting for his next interviewee, "It seems our boy was leading quite a double life. Senatorial aide and dip. All of these wallets and purses are from animals registered here at the hotel. He wasn't on the ship so he didn't have an opportunity to work that crowd. We need to find out whether his boss was in on the take. Octavius tells us the Senator is hard up for money and facing litigation over falsification of documents and legislative testimony. He was hoping to hit up the Bearoness and this Ms. Muskrat. No joy!"

Fetlock Holmes nodded. "This widens our suspect list. Paul may have been killed by someone who caught him lifting their wallet or shoulder bag. I gather he was quite nasty and aggressive. Whoever did him in must have been pretty powerful. Sergeant, what do we know about those gorilla bodyguards of Ms. Muskrat? They operate in th U.S. mostly?"

"Yessir! No form, sir. They're clean and they're licensed. Been in the protective business for years. Of course, that doesn't mean there couldn't be a first time. Our boy may have been quite upset at being turned down by the zillionairess and went after her. The gorillas may have defended her. If they broke his neck and tossed him in the bay, they might be reluctant to fess up. And they sure took off rapidly from the resort They're still down at Abeardeen with an impounded airplane."

Fetlock Holmes whickered. "Not for much longer, I fear. She's pulling strings through the American Consulate to get the plane released and their passports returned. That female rodent packs a lot of weight in international and U.S. government circles with her fortune. But somehow, I don't believe they are guilty. She's strong but not the strong-arm type. I may be wrong but seldom am."

The Border Collie flicked his ears and said, "Why don't we have the Senator in here. He's making all sorts of cooperative noises which I frankly mistrust. See if you can get Octavius and his security people down here at the same time.

*****

"I'm convinced, Bel. He remembered just about all the trivia I threw at him. He looks like you and your DNA tests came up trumps. Say hello to your twin."

"Thanks Donna, That invitation to come to Polar Paradise still holds. I think you'd love it here. OK. Barton, welcome back to the family. Come and meet the rest of the Octavians. And then, you, Octavius and I can discuss what comes next. I assume you want something from us and I can guess what it is."

". I'm not looking for a handout like that scammer Polonius. I want a job!"

The Great Bear chuckled. "We have a few of those available. I gather you're not happy with what you're doing. Technical sales?"

"It's a dead end. The pay's not that great and I'm not crazy about New Jersey. Too expensive. My boss is a jerk. I understand UUI is a great place to work. That computing lab of yours in Kentucky sounds terrific."

"I'll put you in touch with Senhor L. Condor, our CTO. He may have something. But, before I do. I have a question for you. Did you kill Paul Polar?"

Barton looked shocked. "Absolutely not. Are you joking?'

"No, I'm quite serious.'

"Look, Paul was an obnoxious twit in his own right and the fact that he was supporting Polonius only made it worse but I don't just go round offing animals because I don't like them. If I did, I would have killed a lot of them by now."

"Did you know he was also a pickpocket?"

"No, I didn't but I'm not surprised. Any thing to make a buck. The Senator's a fraud and he was a thief. What a money grubbing combo! I suppose your police buddies will be investigating me."

"They will and they are but as usual, you're innocent till proven guilty. OK, come and meet the gang."

He led Barton into the anteroom and I did the introductions, assisted by a glass of champagne. Belinda, still somewhat wary, shook his paw. The others did the same. Chita nailed it. "Welcome, Barton! I guess you'll be another Octavian. It doesn't hurt…much!" Laughs all around.

Ursula called Octavius. He listened for a moment. "Howard, you and I have a date with the detectives. Polonius will be there. Time for some truth telling. Assuming he knows how."

Chapter Twelve

Solar Seas made the choice not to sell.
And the ship's maiden voyage has gone well.
Since the muskrat is gone
They can now carry on
With their deal with our Bearoness Bel.

Aboard the **North Wind** making its way out of the Skagerrak Strait from Oslo and back across the North Sea on its return trip to the Shetlands and Polar Paradise: The Solar Seas executives minus Wally Wapiti who had remained behind at the resort were gathered at lunch in a conference room near the ship's Lodi deck.

Bill Beaver, the COO, was finishing off a sandwich, waving his paws and leading the discussion. "Well, I'll openly admit I was wrong. This cruise has been highly successful so far. We've picked up some passengers both in Copenhagen and Oslo who want to go to Polar Paradise or back to New York. And we have to pick up the group we left off at the Shetlands resort. We'll be heading back just about full. Let's hope this isn't a one time deal. Next month's run is pretty well booked. Let's see what happens."

The CFO Carla Chinchilla nodded. "I hope that murder doesn't sour things. Happily, none of the ship's customers were involved. Everyone's safe and sound although we did have a minor dustup in Copenhagen. A couple of stupid cats got drunk and had a fight."

Pablo Puma, the Corporate Security Officer said, "We don't know for a fact that one of our pax *(passengers)* wasn't involved in the murder. Remember, some of them stayed behind at the Castle. The victim was a fly-in but the perp could have been one of ours. From what I've been picking up from the resort, the police haven't arrested anyone yet."

Carla asked, "Pablo, who was the victim, exactly?"

"A Polar male named Paul. He was the personal secretary to that Alaskan Senator, Polonius Polar Black. Made himself very unpopular with his big sarcastic mouth. I guess he shot it off once too often."

Emilia Emu, the Attorney, winced. "We certainly don't need that kind of publicity. Neither does the Bearoness. Doctor Bear's group, the Octavians, are famous for solving crimes. Even their juvenile twins have been involved in tracking down lawbreakers. And there's that legendary detective, Fetlock Holmes. I understand he's there with the Shetland Yard Chief Superintendent. They may have it solved by the time we reach Polar Paradise."

Carla sighed. "I wonder how Wally is doing. On our last call, he said he found a pub he wants to add to our itinerary. Something to do with a Lion and can you believe it, a Unicorn. This I have to see. I'm sure he's relieved that Ellen Muskrat is off our case. She can be a terror."

Bill Beaver laughed. "I wouldn't want to deal with those gorilla bodyguards of hers. What do you think. Did they kill off Mr. Big Mouth?"

Carla shrugged. "I wouldn't put it past them. Well, let's go see the Captain and get a status report. The cruise has been very smooth so far. Let's hope it stays that way."

*****

"Gentlebeasts, come in, come in." Fetlock Holmes greeted Octavius and Howard. Polonius was with them. They had picked him up on the way to the conference room. "Senator, we have a few more questions for you but first, I think Doctors Bear and Where have some information they want to share."

Octavius waved a paw in the porcupine's direction. Howard coughed. "It concerns you, Senator. We have incontrovertible scientific proof that your are not Bearoness Belinda's father. In fact, you're not related in any way."

108

"What kind of nonsense is this. I am the sow's parent."

Octavius snorted, "No, you're not, sir. We conducted a series of DNA profiles on you and compared them to Bel's. You don't even come close. Your claim to paternity is a fake."

"How dare you! How did you conduct a genetic profile match without my knowledge?'

"An unfinished drink and a few strands clipped from your fur."

"I have a mind to sue you, Doctor Bear."

"That would just expose you to further accusations of fraud. You have several of them on record already. It wouldn't get you any money, either. Sorry but the jig is up on your attempt to get cash out of us or Ms. Muskrat. She's not someone to get angry and you lied to her shamelessly. You might want to consider just going quietly and disappearing."

Superintendent Wardlaw barked. "Not so fast. We still have the issue of your murdered assistant. I regret to inform you, Polonius Black, that you are a major suspect."

"This is too much! I am a United States Senator. You can't hold or arrest me."

"Oh yes, we can. You're already under an indictment back in your native Alaska. You're specifically charged with making false statements on your financial disclosure forms for calendar years 2016 to 2020. The indictment alleges that, during each of those years, you knowingly failed to report receipt of anything of value from companies or individuals, despite the fact that the forms required you to report receipt of such things of value."

"As set forth in the indictment, the Ethics in Government Act requires all members of the United States Senate to file a financial disclosure form, detailing specified financial transactions that the elected official engaged in during the prior calendar year, including disclosure of gifts over a specified monetary amount and disclosure of liabilities in excess of $10,000 owed during any point of a calendar year. The indictment is part of an ongoing federal criminal investigation in the state of Alaska."

Polonius retorted. " An indictment is merely an allegation. Defendants are presumed innocent until and unless proven guilty in a court of law."

"Senator, under UK and US law, we can arrest you if we have strong suspicions that you are guilty of murder. We're not quite at that stage yet but we don't want you to leave these premises until we've determined your innocence."

"My Ambassador and your Foreign and Home Offices are going to hear from me immediately. I'll have my secretary, Paul, on the wire to them as soon as we end this comedy."

"May I remind you that Paul is dead, sir."

"Yes, well. ahem, I'll have to do it myself, then. You have overstepped yourselves and I will see to it that you are penalized severely. Outrageous!"

"Let us change the subject for a moment. It would be in your best interest if you could provide us with any information leading to your assistant's murder."

"Well, I was astonished to discover he was a pickpocket. I knew nothing about that. Any one of his victims could have caught him and done him in."

"We're following up on that as we speak. Tell us about your relationship with him."

"So, are you now accusing me of killing my secretary?"

"As I said, you are in the pool of suspects. You had means and opportunity. We're not sure about motive."

"Well, I didn't like him much but he was efficient and intelligent. He had many helpful contacts and good ideas. So I put up with him. I had no motive to kill him. What about that muskrat and her gorillas? And those cruise line passengers and crew? As I said, he could be quite abrasive. And to repeat myself, he was a pickpocket. Put them in your pool of suspects and leave me out of it. What about this Barton fellow claiming to be Belinda's brother. Did you profile him?"

"In fact we did and he's Belinda's twin. We're questioning him further."

"Do so! As far as I'm concerned, this meeting is over." He stomped out of the room.

Octavius laughed. "He gotten a lot of practice being angered on the Senate floor. That was quite a performance!"

Holmes whickered, "I've seen better. Our lords, nobles, ministers and MPs are all quite well trained in the art of outrage and insult. What say you, Superintendent?"

"He's still on my list. I don't trust him about anything. After all, he's being investigated for financial chicanery."

Octavius chuckled again. "So is half the US government. I suspect the UK is no better."

Wardlaw sighed. "You're probably right.

The Super's cell phone rang. "Wardlaw here."

The voice on the other end was terse. "This is Sir Gregory Goat at the Foreign Office. We have just instructed the Home Office and Shetland Yard to release Ms. Ellen Muskrat's aircraft and return her and her associates' travel documentation. They are to be allowed to leave our shores without any further delay. You fellows have certainly set off a storm up there. The lady swings a lot of clout. The US Ambassador intervened. If you find anything sufficient to warrant an arrest, we shall have to pursue extradition. It will not be easy. She has an army of lawyers here, in most major countries and in the States. Just hope your killer has less influence."

Wardlaw laughed. "You mean like a US Senator?"

"Oh gawd! Do you have one of those, too? Who else is up there at that windswept citadel?"

"Well, a zillionaire bear and his Bearoness mate own the place. Thank the Lord, they're not suspects. *(He winked at Octavius.)* I'm not sure who else of the good and the great we have here. Gilbert and Sullivan were spot on. 'A policeman's lot is not a happy one.' Thanks, Sir Gregory. Go and lick your wounds."

He shook his head. "Thank you, Octavius and Doctor Watt. We'll talk again shortly. Regards to the Bearoness." He turned to the sergeant. "Who's next on our interview list

They decided to interview Wally Wapiti once again. They paged him. He was in Baltasound. They also intended to speak to the Solar Seas Management Committee to see if there were any relationships they missed during the first round. Paul eagerly wanted in on the transaction with Ms. Muskrat. Were any of the ship company's executives negotiating on the side to sell the ship and its route with or without Polar Paradise being in the mix? Of course, they'd have to wait for the *North Wind* to return to Polar Paradise from its tour of Norway and Denmark to get answers to that question.

Meanwhile they had scheduled a Zoom session with the Medical Examiner. He had just completed a more detailed post mortem. The Polar was struck in the neck with a blunt instrument or object. Probably tossed in the bay after his death. No signs of drowning. No alcohol, poison or narcotics. Scratches on front legs and face. In short, evidence of a fight that Paul lost. Any residual hairs or skin from his assailant had washed away in the water. Certainly nothing dispositive.

Whoever had killed him had to be strong enough, tall enough and armed. Perhaps a club or the stock of a rifle or shotgun. So far, they had not found a weapon. It's probably on the bottom of the bay. Or maybe not.

Chapter Thirteen

The Great Bear and his Consort hold court.
And Ms. Ursula's story is short.
Barton's good as he looks.
The Alaskans are crooks.
And she'll give the police her report.

"So, what did you find, Ursula?"

"Plenty and nothing. Polonius is really a senator who may be liable to lose his seat in the next election. The Justice Department, IRS and assorted legislative committees are all staging inquiries into his testimonies, fraud, special deals and influence peddling. There's a good chance he will be prosecuted and he can kiss his nomination goodbye. The Alaskan media are running polls on him and they don't look favorable. He needs money for his campaign and his defense lawyers. His PAC doesn't seem to be raising very much. The sales commission he was to get from Ellen Muskrat would have made a big difference. I think he expected you, Bearoness, to be a pushover and welcome him with open arms. As we now know, he's not your father. Where he got the idea for that scam, I don't know. Possibly his secretary. Of course, it didn't happen and his world is currently in tatters"

"What about the late and unlamented Paul?"

"A nasty piece of work as we continue to discover. I strongly suspect he was blackmailing Polonius about some of his shady dealings. He found any number of ways to make a buck ranging from selling senate votes to picking pockets. I'm afraid the number of high level animals he cheated runs in the hundreds. I'm surprised he survived as long as he did. Oddly enough, his name seldom appears in any of the investigations that are afflicting Polonius. Little or no guilt by association. He was smart. Polonius is a bumptious dope. Clearly, Paul was the brains behind the Senator's crooked activities but he managed to keep his skirts relatively clean. Until now.

"Last but I doubt, not least, there's Barton."

"Ah yes, Barton. That's what I meant when I said 'nothing'. If he has a dubious past, he has managed to keep it well hidden. He left you and your aunt and after wandering around was taken in by an orphan school. Like you, Bearoness, he's highly intelligent and he managed to win several university scholarships and internships in electronics and information processing. He does indeed work in technical sales for a mid-level consulting firm but has been unhappy with his situation. Uninteresting, low remuneration and no prospects. Plus, his expenses are exceeding his income. No romances that we can find. Never been married and doesn't seem enthused by the prospect. He knew who you were and followed your career. He finally decided to take a short leave and come to you, hat in paw, and ask for your help. It seems we all agree. He is your twin brother. Of course, it's your call how you're going to treat him. As far as Paul's death is concerned, we are reasonably convinced that Barton is no killer."

Octavius responded. "Bel and I agree to give him a chance. I'm setting up an interview with Condo. We'll see if there's a place for him at the Hexagon. And living in Kentucky is cheaper than New Jersey."

*****

Late at night, *The North Wind* slipped past *Belinda's Barge* and into its assigned position next to the quay and travel center at Polar Paradise. Given the time, the Captain forewent blowing the ship's horn and quietly as possible, tied up and lowered the gangways for those few still awake and wanting to go to the Hotel. By prior agreement, the Solar Seas Management Committee was among the several souls debarking.

Wally Wapiti, Octavius, Superintendent Wardlaw, Fetlock Holmes, Lord David, the Wolves, Ms. Fairbearn and I were there to meet them. Octavius greeted the bleary-eyed group and said, "Thanks for joining us here at the castle. We have some questions to ask you about the death of Senator Polonius' secretary but they can wait until morning. Ms. Fairbearn has arranged rooms for you and we'll meet you with a hearty breakfast at nine tomorrow. I hope you can catch some shut-eye and join us ready to discuss the situation."

They looked at the CEO and Emilia Emu asked. "What's this all about, Wally?"

The Superintendent interrupted. "Just trying to close off some open queries, counsellor. We're wondering if any of you can add to our knowledge about how, why, where and when this murder took place. And of course, whodunnit?"

"Ah, so it was a murder, not an accident."

"Yes, we're certain of that. Anyway, pleasant dreams. We'll see you in the AM. Oh. sorry. It's AM already."

The quintet trooped off after the House Manager. We turned and headed back to our beds.

*****

As the sun rose in the Shetlands sky and the cloned sheep wait-staff were clearing away breakfast dishes, Octavius, Wardlaw, Holmes and I were sitting back prepared to listen to anything the Solar Seas execs were willing to contribute. There was only one taker – the COO.

Bill Beaver admitted to meeting with Polonius and Paul when the **North Wind** had first docked at the travel center. "They were trying to get information on our plans to sell the ship and the route to Ellen Muskrat. I told them nothing because I knew nothing. When we were approached by the zillionaire while she was on the ship, we were noncommittal. The Executive Committee was divided on what we should do. Actually, the group, including Wally, opposed the sale. I was the only one in favor, Deadlocked!"

"Anyhow, Paul tried to browbeat us into supporting the sale so they could face down the Bearoness with a fait accompli. It was obvious that

Ellen Muskrat had promised them a substantial fee for swinging the transaction. The two of them didn't realize how dead set Belinda was against selling the resort to anyone, much less the Muskrat. Paul was an arrogant jerk, if you don't mind my speaking ill of the dead. Polonius is no better. I got the distinct impression the Bearoness doesn't believe he is her father. Even if he is, she wants nothing to do with him."

This just confirmed what the detectives already knew or surmised. The rest of Solar Seas management had no contact with the victim and couldn't add anything to the narrative.

Chapter Fourteen

So the Senator shows up to schmooze
With an offer that Bel can't refuse
Much to his great chagrin
She still doesn't give in.
Then he tells her, he can't stand to lose.

Octavius had left the Bearonial Suite to be with the detectives and the cruise line managers. Huntley was down in the Hotel's offices going over the day's activities with Ms. Fairbearn, Harold and me. God only knows where the twins had gotten off to. Belinda was alone in her suite with the exception of the omnipresent Ursula.

A knock on the door. The AGI said. "It's Polonius. Do you want to let him in?"

The Bearoness pawsed and then shrugged her shoulders. "OK, let's see what the old swindler wants." She pressed a button that opened the entrance to the suite. Polonius stood there, upright. He had taken to using a cane recently. His wounds seemed to be bothering him."

"Good morning, daughter!"

"Oh Polonius, don't start! We all know you're not my father. We're not related at all. So, just stop the act. Give it up as a bad job! Who are you, really."

He stared at her. "I'm the Senior Senator from the fair state of Alaska and deserving of some respect, Bearoness." He sneered her title.

"Sorry. I'm not in the mood to be respectful to a dishonest fraud who's under indictment for financial hanky-panky. Are you also guilty of killing your assistant?"

"You insulting sow! I came here to make you an attractive offer. Perhaps I won't."

"Ooh. This is fascinating. What skullduggery do you have in mind?"

"In spite of your Scottish Bearonial status, you're a native of the United States. Specifically Alaska. You have dual citizenship."

"Tell me something I don't know."

"I can make it very profitable for you back in Alaska by getting a franchise authorizing you to build and open another resort in Anchorage or Fairbanks. Polar Paradise West. The cruise company could profit from it as well. Of course, I would expect to be amply compensated for using my influence before I retire."

"You are unbelievable! No thank you! Tell me. Did you ever know my true father?"

"I might as well tell you. Years ago, before I was first elected, your father and I were political cronies. He's dead. Killed in that assassination attempt that left me scarred and limping. It was only recently that Paul discovered you and your exalted position. We needed money. We decided to take full advantage of the so-called relationship. I would pose as your father. That husband of yours and your DNA specialist ruined that."

"Why did you kill Paul?"

"Oh, you figured that out, did you. In addition to being a petty thief, he was a blackmailer. The creep said he would reveal to you and the Muskrat that I was a phony. He threatened to surface a lot of records that would sew up my indictments. I didn't have enough money to meet his demands, so I killed him. Clubbed him with this heavy cane. Just the same way I'm going to get rid of you. You know too much - *daughter*. You'll take an accidental fall off your balcony and I will silently disappear. Those stupid detectives and your husband will have another death to deal with. Those obnoxious twins will lose a mother. So sad! " He laughed.

He lunged at her with his cane. He was bigger than Bel. She picked up a chair and held him off. He didn't realize that Ursula had been monitoring and recording all of this and had summoned Frau Schuylkill and Colonel Wyatt Where along with Ms. Fairbearn, Lord David and his security staff.

Frau Schuylkill and Colonel Where

They ran to the suite. Ms. Fairbearn threw open the door and the two wolves leaped, pounced and toppled the bear. They growled and snapped at his throat. Lord David pointed a pistol at him and two security types grabbed him and bound his front and hind paws. Ursula summoned Octavius, the detectives and Sergeant Byrne. Traveling from the ground floor to the Bearonial Suite in the penthouse took a few minutes but when they arrived, they discovered the situation well in hand.

Superintendent Wardlaw intoned. "Polonius Black, I am arresting you for the murder of your secretary Paul Polar and the attempted murder of Bearoness Belinda Béarnaise Bruin Bear *(nee Black.* You do not have to say anything. Anything you do say may be given in evidence."

"Nonsense. Do you realize who I am? A United States Senator. I want a lawyer. You have no proof of any wrongdoing on my part."

Ursula rang her chime. "Will a confession do?" The large apartment television screen flickered into action and she played back the entire dialogue and struggle between Belinda and the Polar. He stared blankly at the screen and then the lynx in the laptop. "Damn you, Octavius Bear and your electronic folderol."

I grinned. "Can you afford a lawyer?"

119

Epilogue

Now the Senator's going to jail
And the North Wind is ready to sail.
So it's time to tell you
Our adventure is through.
But who knows what the next will entail.

The Police helicopter had arrived and Polonius was hustled aboard on his way to Abeardeen and on to Lerwick for processing, detention and formal prosecution. Things did not look good for the senator, both in Scotland and back in the United States. Fetlock Holmes, Superintendent Wardlaw and Sergeant Byrne joined the prisoner in the chopper after bidding Octavius and Belinda farewell. Holmes neighed and whickered. "Octavius, old boy. You two are supposed to be retired. When are you going to learn the meaning of the word?"

The Great Bear laughed. "Fetlock, you don't realize what it takes to keep all these Octavians occupied. They expect to be part of the Adventure of the Week Club and Bel and I don't want to disappoint them. Fly safely, old friends. Nigel, please keep us posted on this case. It hit a little too closely to home."

They waved as the whirlybird lifted off the heliport surface and headed out to the bay passing over the docked **North Wind** and **Bel's Barge** that was getting ready for another excursion. Harold and the waitresses were busily prepping for the next wave of tourists.

Wally Wapiti and the Solar Seas corporate team had been watching the Police departing with their detainee. He came over to Octavius and Bel, shaking his head and full rack of antlers. "Well, Doctor Bear, nothing like a little excitement to liven up a cruise. Bearoness, I assume our lawyers have reached agreement on our continued relationship. We already have a substantial list of passengers for our cruise next month. Quite a few want to spend time here at Polar Paradise plus Lion and Unicorn's pub. "

Belinda smiled. "We have some fly-in reservations from the States who want to return on the *North Wind.* Wally, I think this is the beginning of a beautiful friendship."

They both laughed. "Thank goodness, Ellen Muskrat is out of the picture. I couldn't stand working with that female. Unlike you, Bearoness."

"Thank you, Wally. My pleasure."

Ursula rang her chime. "I hate to break up this lovefest but you should know, Doctor Bear. Ms. Muskrat has made an offer to buy our Deep Data Hexagon. She wants to invest in AI."

"No interest, Ursula."

Ms. Fairbearn came over in a mighty huff. "I'm glad to see that nasty Polar got his just deserts but do you know. He left without paying his bill."

THE END
The Casebooks of Octavius Bear
Volume 20 —The Case of the Polar Politician

Acknowledgements

These books have evolved over a long period of time and under a wide range of influences and circumstances. I am indebted to many people for helping to bring Octavius and his cohorts to the printed and electronic page. Thanks most especially to my wife, Virginia, for her insights and clever suggestions as well as her unfailing enthusiasm for the project and patience with its author.

To my sons, Mark and Andrew and their spouses, Cynthia and Lorraine, for helping to make these tomes more readable and audience friendly. To Cathy Hartnett, cheerleader-extraordinaire for her eagerness to see this alternate universe take form. To Jack Magan, Paul Bernish, David Lars Chamberlain, Dan Walker, Dan Andriacco, Amy Thomas, Luke Benjamin Kuhns, Derrick Belanger, Kirthana Shivakumar, Raju Chacko and Zohreh Zand for their enthusiastic encouragement. And to all of my generous Kickstarter backers.

Kudos to Jim Effler, the late Bob Gibson and Brian Belanger for their wonderful illustrations and covers. Thanks, of course, to Sharon, Steve and Timi Emecz at MX Publishing for giving The Great Bear and his gang of Octavians a wonderful home.

If, in spite of all this support, some errors or inconsistencies have crept through, the buck stops here. Needless to say, all of the characters, situations, and narratives are fictional. Some locations, devices, historical figures and events are real.

Thanks to Wikipedia for providing facts, figures and pictures used throughout this book.

Also by Harry DeMaio

The Octavius Bear Series – Books 1-20

1-The Open and Shut Case

2-The Case of the Spotted Band

3-The Case of Scotch

4-The Lower Case

5-The Curse of the Mummy's Case

6-The Attaché Case

7-The Suit Case

8-The Crank Case

9-The Basket Case

10-The Camera Case

11-The Wurst Case Scenario

12-The Nut Case

13-A Case of Déjà Vu

14-The Case of Cosmic Chaos

15-A Case for the Birds

16-The Cases Down Under

17-The Octavian Cases

18-The Bear Faced Liar

19-Bears at Sea

20-The Case of the Polar Politician

Sherlock Holmes and the Glamorous Ghost Books 1 – 4; Sherlock Holmes and Solar Pons Pastiches in MX Publishing and Belanger Books Anthologies; Dear Holmes Letter Series-The Indignant Indigent and Agony Anti

About the Author

Harry DeMaio is a ***nom de plume*** of Harry B. DeMaio, successful author of several books on Information Security and Business Networks as well as the twenty-volume ***Casebooks of Octavius Bear.*** His four volume series, ***Sherlock Holmes and the Glamorous Ghost*** has been very well received. He is also a published author of pastiches for Belanger Books and the MX Sherlock Holmes series.

A retired business executive, former consultant, information security specialist, elected official, private pilot, disk jockey and graduate school adjunct professor, he whiles away his time traveling and writing preposterous books, articles and stories.

He has appeared on many radio and TV shows and is an accomplished, frequent public speaker.

Former New York City natives, he and his extremely patient and helpful wife, Virginia, live in Cincinnati (and several other parallel universes.) They have two sons, Mark, living in Scottsdale, Arizona and Andrew. in Cortlandt Manor, New York, both of whom are quite successful and quite normal, thus putting the lie to the theory that insanity is hereditary.

Comments are welcome. Positive or negative, His skin is thick. Of course, positive is better.

His e-mail is hdemaio@zoomtown.com

You can also find him on Facebook.

His website and blog is www.tavighostbooks.com

His books are available on Amazon, Barnes and Noble, the Book Depository and other fine bookstores as well as directly from MX Publishing and Belanger Books.

Milton Keynes UK
Ingram Content Group UK Ltd.
UKHW030855180424
441376UK00007B/253

9 781804 244452